The Unexpected Aneurysm
of the Potato Blossom Queen

The Unexpected Aneurysm
of the Potato Blossom Queen

Garrett Socol

atmosphere press

Table of Contents

To Sheryl & Marc

The Annual Company Christmas Party

The thought of her husband Mitch in love with her colleague Cynthia danced in Katie's head even though she tried to convince herself nothing was going on behind her back. Five nights later, she was officially told what was going on behind her back, and it was precisely what had been dancing in her head. From that moment on, she preferred being unconscious.

Katie Noonan's favorite time of day had become nine at night when she would swallow the magical tablets Dr. Sappington had prescribed. She knew she'd be asleep within half an hour or so, and those thirty minutes were bliss. Cozy in a plush, magnificent limo heading to the airport, this was a velvet carpet ride of comfort and anticipation. At the twenty-eight-minute mark, she'd be on the aircraft, seat buckled, ready for take-off into the starry, expansive sky. Then she would sleep luxuriously late into the following morning.

Katie. Never Katherine. Her parents called her Katie as did her friends, co-workers and husband of two years before he met Cynthia Hook. Cynthia. Never Cindy. The marriage wasn't perfect; something seemed to be missing like the final piece of a complex jigsaw puzzle. But she truly loved Mitch, and he seemed to love her back. She assumed the relationship would improve with age like fine wine and 401(k)s.

Katie didn't blame herself for the miscarriage of the marriage. Why *shouldn't* she have taken her husband to the company Christmas party? That was what employees did. Dozens dragged their husbands and wives and significant others to the annual bash without a single negative repercussion; it was not considered a marriage-threatening action.

The employees who worked together eight to ten hours a day were a family of sorts; some spent more time with their colleagues than they did with their spouses. They knew one another's likes, dislikes, interests, habits, senses of style or lack thereof, senses of humor or lack thereof. But they were relatively ignorant when it came to the subject of intimate relations. Only during the annual company party, when partners were expected to appear, did private lives become public as if the information was being disseminated in a company-wide e-mail.

It was the *women* who did the gossiping. The men were too busy downing hard liquor to ward off the discomfort of socializing with perfect strangers. The big surprises of the night were that Elsa Keck's husband was a man twice her age and Neal Mundle's partner was a man. Some people had suspected Neal's sexual orientation, but no one was entirely sure until he brought his tall, tuxedo-clad partner to the party. "Gay men are so well groomed," Katie remarked to her still-handsome husband.

Standing a few feet away, Cynthia Hook (Director of Media & Partnerships) couldn't help overhearing. She also couldn't help noticing the still-handsome husband. "Isn't that the truth?" she interjected. "So well dressed and polite."

Introductions were made to the respective spouses of Katie and Cynthia. Bruno Hook was a gaunt man with a mass of jet-black hair and a treacherous glint in his eye. In a too-tight black suit, there was something sleazy about him, as if he were capable of committing a felony one day and forgetting about it the next. To Katie, he seemed reptilian.

Katie politely excused herself from the foursome, eager to enjoy two solid minutes away from the bright lights and blaring music.

Examining herself in the large ornate mirror in the ladies' room, she wished her hazel eyes were bigger, nose smaller, and lips fuller. But her chestnut-colored hair was lustrous, and her body was in terrific shape thanks to her sadistic personal trainer who, she was certain, had been a Gestapo officer in a previous life. She reapplied her rose-red lipstick—this gave her small mouth a little pizzazz—and strolled out of the room with a bit more confidence than she'd had going in. Little did she know that Bruno had excused himself only seconds after Katie had excused *herself*, leaving Cynthia and Mitch alone. When Katie returned to the spot where they'd been standing, none of the original four was there. She found this considerably disconcerting.

Glancing around the large banquet room, everyone from the Chicago advertising agency looked familiar, though their attire seemed peculiar and out of place. The young females (who often wore jeans and tank tops to the office) opted for glittering party dresses and designer pumps. The young males (who usually wore torn jeans and T-shirts to work) donned button-down dress shirts with expensive neckties executed in lame Windsor knots.

Champagne, liquor, and surprisingly potent cider rum punch flowed freely and plentifully. Unfortunately, some of the reticent employees became loose and loud after a few cocktails. As for the *ordinarily* loose and loud staff members, they became obnoxious and offensive. Two employees, one an account director, the other an assistant in Strategic Development, had to be escorted out the door by security.

Bruno finally returned from the men's room. "Hey," he said to Katie. "Where's my battle-ax?"

"I don't know any battle-ax," she replied with annoyance. His crassness made her cringe. "I don't know where Mitch is either."

"Didn't see him in the men's room."

They stood side by side, hoping their spouses would magically appear. But magic didn't happen. "What do you do at the agency?" Bruno asked, less out of interest and more out of filling the awkward silence.

"Creative director."

"Sounds impressive."

"Thanks," Katie replied. She had no interest whatsoever in hearing about Bruno's line of work, if there *was* one, so she remained mum.

Three minutes passed, and then five. "Maybe they're getting another drink," Bruno suggested. "Let's check."

He led Katie to the bar, but the spouses were nowhere in sight. Katie began to experience panicky palpitations, the kind she felt when discovering a summons for jury duty in her mailbox. She began chewing her bottom lip.

Adjacent to the main banquet area with its booming music and blinding Christmas lights was a more intimate room for those who preferred quiet. The vanilla-scented votive candles, along with the soothing music and plush velvet furniture, created a tranquil, comforting ambience, perfect for those seeking romance or nursing a migraine. "I'll bet they're in there," Katie said.

When she and Bruno entered the space, they instantly spotted their spouses sitting cozily in a dark aqua banquette near the flickering fireplace. Mitch and Cynthia seemed engrossed in conversation and in each other.

"What do you suppose they're talking about?" Bruno asked.

"Could be anything," Katie responded, trembling slightly. "Ad revenues. Alimony payments. Travel. Mitch has been wanting to go to Peru."

"So why don't you go?"

"Because I'd rather go to *Peoria*. Let's join the duo, shall we?"

As they approached, Katie's suspicious eyes darted from Mitch to Cynthia and back. When Mitch saw his wife, his face lit up, but Katie didn't buy it. Insincerity oozed from his eyes; it was obvious he resented the interruption. "Did you know Cynthia speaks three languages?" he asked.

"English and Spanish," Katie said. "What else?"

"French," Mitch told her.

"You don't speak French," Katie said to her colleague.

"She looks at the pictures in Paris Match," Bruno chimed in. "That's about it."

"I do not just look at the pictures." she stated in a huffy tone. "I *read*. I happen to speak la langue tres bien, merci."

"Your wife tells me you want to go to Peru," Bruno said to Mitch.

"I *do* want to go to Peru," he replied. "I've never been to South Africa." Immediately he realized his faux pas. "South *America!* Sorry."

"Peru seems like a colorful place," Cynthia said. "The one in South America."

"Well, Bruno, why don't you take your wife on a South American adventure?" Katie suggested. "Sooner rather than later."

"Why sooner?" Cynthia asked.

"Because you never know what might happen to put a kibosh on your exciting excursion," she explained. "On the drive home from tonight's party, for example, you might be barreling down the highway, humming along to some benign music on the radio, and suddenly you're hit head-on by a drunk driver zooming at ninety miles per hour in the wrong direction. It's happened, you know."

Katie's gruesome tale of what could possibly take place generated dropped jaws and a macabre silence. "Well," Cynthia finally said, staring at Katie, "thank you for sharing that lovely scenario." Katie held Cynthia's gaze for what seemed like a significant length of time before looking away. With a keen instinct and a sickening stomach, she wondered if Mitch and Cynthia had made some quick plan for a clandestine rendezvous later in the week.

"Don't look now," Cynthia whispered. "But Ruby Abrams just jumped on top of the piano. Dear God, please don't let her sing."

The robust, red-haired sixty-year-old was the agency's Brand Strategist who also happened to be a self-proclaimed cabaret singer. Nick Pomphrey from Graphic Design began to play a few notes on the piano, and Ruby started singing "You're the Top." Though she had a decent voice, she was no Patti LuPone. Halfway through the Cole Porter number, she forgot the lyrics and tried to wing it, but the performance quickly turned into an embarrassment. "One jumbo glass of punch too many," she joked into the microphone. "It'll get you every time."

Cynthia leaned over to Katie and whispered in her ear. "How can she face anyone Monday morning?"

"Takes guts," Katie replied. "She looks like she belongs in Madame Tussauds."

Just then, poor Ruby plunged off the piano with a loud, painful thud. "Are you all right?" Roland Shreeve shouted as he rushed to her rescue.

Ruby emitted a raucous cackle to signal that she was fine. "Takes more than *that* to crack these old bones."

"Should we call an ambulance?" Kit Herzog from Human Resources asked.

"No ambulance!" the would-be songbird howled. "I was just in the hospital for an endoscopic retrograde cholangiopancreatography and I'm not going back anytime soon!" Two guys from Studio Operations helped her to her swollen feet. "See? Still in one jolly piece," she said.

"Her body fat must've eased the impact, like falling onto a mattress," Cynthia quietly said.

"Merry Christmas, everybody!" Ruby shouted with all her strength.

The end of the night turned out to be ten interminable minutes later. The couples waited silently for the valet to fetch their cars in the cold night air.

Katie and Mitch barely spoke on the drive home except to discuss Cynthia Hook. "She seems like a great gal," Mitch said.

"Great gal?" Katie asked, surprised.

"Congenial," he said.

"On the contrary," Katie stated. "She can be quite unpleasant."

"I found her to be pleasant."

"You don't know her well, Mitch. Believe me, she's cutthroat and nasty, offensive and rude."

For the rest of the night, something gnawed at Katie like a tingling itch she couldn't reach. The following day, the tingling became more intense, more bothersome. The tingle took shape like a bud evolving into a begonia: the thought of Mitch madly in love with the demonic Cynthia. This nightmarish notion danced in Katie's head even though she valiantly tried to convince herself nothing was going on behind her back.

Five anxious nights later, Katie learned what was going on behind her back.

"Can't keep it to myself any longer," Mitch admitted. "I've been seeing Cynthia Hook the past few nights."

Mitch took no enjoyment in keeping secrets. But in this particular situation, he was proud of himself for delaying the revelation as long as he did, for keeping the emotional pain away from his wife an extra few days.

Katie felt nauseated but she couldn't run to the bathroom because she needed the truth more than a toilet. "Are you in love with her?" she inquired with trepidation. Almost immediately she got her answer; it was the miniscule pause that gave it away.

"Uh, well," Mitch mumbled, "Yeah, I guess so.... No, I'm *sure* about it. Yes, we're in love. Madly, recklessly, thrillingly in love."

"*One* adverb would've sufficed."

"She's telling Bruno tonight. Right now, in fact."

"Oh, so this was planned, like a finely tuned attack, an ambush. *Inform the spouses at the exact same time.* I've never seen you arrange something so meticulously. Is she telling him in Spanish or French?"

"Very funny," Mitch said.

Katie needed a minute to think clearly, to breathe normally, to recover from this catastrophic jolt.

"Well," she finally said as calmly as possible, "as your wife, all I ever wanted was for you to be happy. So, I guess Cynthia helped make me the perfect spouse. I delivered happiness to your fucking doorstep."

Now, in the aftermath of this heinous, monstrous tsunami, there was silence. Mitch quietly wandered off to sleep in the guest room while Katie rushed to the bathroom and threw up with aplomb. Ladylike vomiting. Nothing violent, nothing volcanic, not like she was attempting to rid her body of some alien entity. The retching of a royal.

As she lay awake between very brief intervals of sleep, Katie realized that a divorce was imminent and that Mitch reneged on the sacred pledge of allegiance he'd made to his bride. He was a man for whom deception was second nature. He was an insensitive prick.

The following morning at the office, Cynthia avoided Katie like an opportunistic infection. Unfortunately, just before noon, they found themselves facing one another in the long west hallway. "I'm sorry for the way things turned out," Cynthia said in a slightly condescending manner. "But once in a while, something life changing happens, and you have no control."

"Horse crap," Katie shot back, enraged. "You have control over everything you do. You can feel something but choose something else. It might hurt for six months or so, but you'd get over it, especially if it was the right decision. In any case, let's drop it, shall we?"

"Absolutely," Cynthia replied. "We'll deal with each other as if nothing out of the ordinary took place."

"Right. We'll go about our daily routine, and if we happen to encounter one another in the break room or at a staff meeting, we'll smile politely and pretend we don't notice everyone whispering behind our backs."

"You're welcome to go out with Bruno, by the way," Cynthia offered.

"I'd rather go out with a gorilla," she snapped. "Or a prison escapee."

"There's no reason to be bitter," Cynthia said.

"Oh, there's *every* reason," Katie emphatically stated, "I came *this close* to staying home from the party," she said, illustrating a length of one inch with two fingers.

"That close?" Cynthia inquired with stupefaction.

"That close," Katie confirmed.

"Well," Cynthia said with faux sincerity, "I hope the rest of your holiday season is filled with oodles of cheer."

A painful silence followed as Katie peered at her nemesis with pure and utter hatred. Then Cynthia turned away and lunged past Katie, sashaying down the hallway.

The marriage of Katie and Mitch was now history because of one measly inch. But one inch of *what?* Vegetable? Animal? Mineral? Or was it something more oblique, like indecision? Fear? Discomfort?

A social event, this holiday party was called, but it was a business meeting, really. Nobody wanted to socialize with these people in their uncomfortable semi-formal attire as they nibbled on spicy tuna tartare. Everyone would've preferred to stay home and watch Netflix while stuffing their faces with junk food. But it was almost a requirement to attend the holiday bash. If one didn't show up, one would've had to supply a very convincing excuse the following Monday morning.

"Damn that holiday party," Katie muttered between clenched teeth as she leaned against the wall. "Damn it, damn it, damn it to hell."

"Damn *what* to hell?" the throaty female voice asked.

Katie quickly turned around to find Ruby Abrams approaching her in the hallway.

"Damn that damn company Christmas party."

"I heard about Captain Hook and your hubby," Ruby said with compassion. "Just remember, kiddo: When a man is stolen, the wife is new meat on the market—100% choice beef. Juicy, delectable, in great demand."

"Thanks," she said.

Ruby gave Katie a quick, warm embrace. Then she strolled away like a diva approaching an enthusiastic coterie of fans.

*

"If it hadn't been the Christmas party, it would have been something else," Dr. Sappington explained to Katie a few days later. "The marriage wasn't strong. You *knew* that."

"Still, he ripped me open, Dr. Sappington. Grabbed a chunk of me and seared it like a steak. Now my favorite time of day is nine at night when I take my sleeping pill and drift off to a place in which Cynthia Hook and Mitch Noonan do not exist."

"You can't escape in sleep. You won't find peace or happiness by avoiding life. You need to find a solution in your conscious world."

"I don't know if that's possible."

"I think it is," Dr. Sappington said. "You're a successful, intelligent woman. And you've always been resourceful. I guarantee you'll think of something to fill the void."

"Do you honestly believe that?" she asked.

"I honestly do."

You'll think of something. For the rest of the day, for the rest of the month, the words of her shrink reverberated in Katie's head. *You'll think of something.*

It took exactly six weeks for Katie to think of something.

It took her almost ten months to execute.

*

Straight-laced, conservative Katie Noonan took to the streets at night, gradually becoming familiar with the sordid side of big city life. To her astonishment, she discovered an underground world of romance for rent and sex for sale—men and women, straight, gay, and everything in between, hustlers and hookers and drug dealers huddled in dark alleys. It was not a world in which she felt the least bit comfortable, but never once did she falter from her plan.

She learned of a bar in which high-class hookers were known to frequent. One late Wednesday night, Katie grabbed a stool and ordered a ginger ale from the balding bartender. To her right sat a glamorous redhead with a bosom that cried out to be noticed (it didn't take many tears). To her left sat a truly stunning brunette in a ruffled strapless scarlet mini dress that left little to the imagination. Katie was wearing a conservative black sheath dress that left *everything* to the imagination. She couldn't help admiring the brunette's sizzling outfit and wondering what the price tag was. To her astonishment, the tag was actually showing. And she was certain the woman wasn't aware of this.

"Excuse me," Katie said. "I have to compliment you on your sensational dress. I love the style and color."

"Thank you, honey. I wish I could return the compliment, but you're dressed for a funeral."

Katie chuckled. "Pretty awful, huh? I know. But as far as *your* stunning dress is concerned, I have to tell you that the price tag is showing."

"Are you kidding me?" Violet asked, mortified.

"I wouldn't kid about something like that."

"You are one observant chick," she whispered in a panic. "I'm off to the loo."

When Violet returned a few moments later, sans price tag, she seemed relaxed and confident. "In my entire life that has never happened. You saved me a heap of embarrassment."

"What are new friends for?"

"Absolutely. Name?"

"Katie. Yours?"

"Violet. You're not working, are you?" she asked.

"Uh, no," Katie stated. "I'm not. But I think there's absolutely nothing wrong with women who do."

"Glad to have your blessing."

Katie bought the drinks and Violet downed the vodka martinis. Several men tried to grab Violet's attention, but she ignored them. She was enjoying her girl talk too much. After almost an hour of laughs and conversation, Violet asked, "What exactly are you doing here, honey?"

"Well," Katie began, deliberately lowering the volume of her voice to a virtual whisper, "I'm organizing a little project that will pay quite well. Trust me—I have a lot of money to spend."

"Sounds intriguing," Violet said, crossing one long shapely leg over the other. "How can I be of help?"

"In a nutshell," Katie said in a conspiratorial way, "I need to find a magnificent looking man, someone in your profession, and I have no idea where to look."

"I know my share of gents," Violet said.

"But he has to be drop-dead gorgeous. Body of Thor. Not only should he stop traffic, he should cause accidents. When he enters a room, every female eye should zero in on him and *stay* on him no matter what else is happening. *That's* how sexy and charismatic he needs to be."

"I'm getting the picture."

"I can't stress that enough," Katie said. "He has to be the kind of guy women leave their husbands for. Do you understand? *Women leave their husbands for.*"

"Tall order," Violet said. "But a few come to mind. One of them actually met a woman who left her husband of ten years for him."

"Are they still together?"

Violet laughed out loud. "It was just a *job* for him, honey."

"He's the one I want," Katie said with mounting

excitement. "Jaw-droppingly beautiful?"

"Jaws and drawers will drop, I guarantee," Violet assured her. "You're lonely and divorced?"

"Oh, no no no, it's not for me," Katie insisted.

"Then who is it for?" she asked. "And what exactly would this Adonis have to do?"

Katie took a deep, thoughtful breath and leaned into Violet. "I work at a successful advertising agency. And next month there's going to be this big company Christmas party…"

*

The female employees were gossiping and comparing party dresses. The men were downing Santa Clausmopolitans and Rudolph's Tipsy Spritzers to ward off the discomfort of socializing with perfect strangers. In the festive atmosphere, the big surprises of the night were that Francesca Russo's partner was a heavily pierced, tattooed biker chick who zoomed in on a Harley-Davidson, and Bryan Frogget's new wife was an exotic beauty from the Philippines, young enough to be his daughter. This was the company's annual Christmas party.

When Katie arrived with Blayze Davis on her arm, the energy in the room turned electric. The eyes of every female in attendance (and more than a few males) instantly focused on Blayze. Conversations came to an abrupt halt.

Movie-star handsome with the body of an underwear model, Blayze Davis had bedroom eyes the color of the Aegean and a smile that could melt ice. He and Katie headed to the crowded bar where Cynthia and Mitch were getting soused on the popular cocktails of the evening. Within sixty seconds, Katie felt a light touch on her shoulder. "Merry Christmas, Katie."

"Right back in your face," Katie replied.

"Mitch and I were just commenting on how lovely you look tonight."

"Well, thank you very much," she replied. "I'd like you to meet my friend Blayze Davis. Blayze, this is my ex-husband Mitch Noonan and Cynthia Hack."

"Hook," Cynthia said, gazing intensely at Blayze.

"Yes *Hook*, I'm sorry."

With deliberation, Blayze unleashed the full force of his seductive grin on Cynthia. She ate it up like a starving activist who just decided to end a hunger strike.

The foursome engaged in superficial chitchat for a while, discussing favorite Christmas flicks, Cambodian genocide under the Khmer Rouge, and the town's hottest New Year's Eve parties they'd like to crash. Then Katie said, "I wonder if I could have a word with you, Mitch." She turned to Cynthia. "Would you mind if I borrowed him for a bit?"

"Not at all, be my guest," Cynthia said with pleasure. "I'll stay here and become acquainted with Blayze." She was experiencing an acute case of tunnel vision, and at the end of the tunnel was Blayze Davis, smiling back.

"Don't look so woebegone," Katie said to Mitch as she escorted him away. "We'll be back in ten or twenty minutes."

When Katie and Mitch were gone, Cynthia literally latched onto Blayze and didn't let go.

"I love your name," she remarked. "Blayze. It suits

you."

"Thank you," Blayze replied. (He didn't confess that the name on his birth certificate was Bruce Dibble.)

"You're certainly on fire. And I'm sure I'm not the *only* one who feels the heat."

This was the beginning of a carefully arranged match and the end of Cynthia and Mitch.

This introduction also gave birth to a series of lunchtime trysts that were unlike anything Cynthia had ever experienced. Every day just after noon, the calculating charmer arrived at Cynthia's office where he made passionate love to her in her heavily locked, dimly lit corner office, sometimes in her walk-in closet, sometimes atop her cluttered desk. When she could get away from Mitch in the evening, she and Blayze enjoyed clandestine rendezvous in upscale hotel rooms, all adorned with colorful Christmas lights. Cynthia luxuriated in Blayze's perfectly sculpted body as it took on a red holiday glow like the Hope Diamond when exposed to ultraviolet rays.

Then Cynthia made it official: She was leaving Mitch after exactly twelve months.

Of course, Blayze was only planning to stay with Cynthia for exactly ten more days. That was all Katie could afford.

It was the best ten days of Cynthia's life.

It was the worst ten days of Mitch's life.

It was the best investment Katie had ever made.

The Fedora

Exactly two days after her twelfth birthday, Shawna Deardorf's exceedingly tall father hung himself in the guest bathroom of the family's two-story, five-bedroom house. Because of his height, it was perplexing to the police how he managed to accomplish this in such a small space. The conclusion was that he must've bent his legs or touched his chest with his knees as he inhaled his final breath.

The day before this stupefying, crushing event, Charley Deardorf spoke to his daughter as though she were an adult. "When you meet someone and fall in love, don't let him go, no matter what the circumstance." They were leisurely strolling through their postcard-perfect New England neighborhood on a cloudy August afternoon. Charley seemed content, *happy* even; he cherished the time he spent with his only child.

"What if the person I love is mean to me?" she inquired.

"That's a cue that you should walk away. Fast."

"What if he wants me to join a religious cult?" she asked.

"Your answer would be an emphatic no."

"What if he wants us to join the circus?"

"You'd have to think long and hard about a life of snake charming, stilt walking and flying trapezes, not to mention huge heaps of elephant dung."

From Shawna's point of view, it seemed as if her father had taken *her* life along with his. Every holiday memory, every weekend getaway, every word of encouragement came from this man. Her eccentric, draconian mother, Claire, wasn't quite as devoted to the family patriarch. "Your father was troubled," she said. "A terribly troubled soul."

"Do you mean his moods?"

"That was part of it. Those gray periods grabbed him by the throat like the Boston Strangler. I had a feeling it would end this way, though not in the guest bathroom."

"Where did you think it would end?" Shawna asked.

"The master bedroom," Claire concluded. "Your father loved that room—his framed diplomas, French Provincial furniture. There was nothing he enjoyed more than lounging in bed with a good spy novel and a bottle of Courvoisier. If he'd been able to, he would've stayed in that room all day. Instead, he died down the hall at dusk."

The afternoon of the funeral was an uncommonly cool and windy one for late summer. The grievers who gathered were clutching their scarves, sweaters, and jackets tightly, fearful that the garments might fly into the sky, never to return to terra firma. Shawna recognized everyone in attendance except a statuesque woman in a double-breasted trench coat and black felt fedora. "Who's that tall lady in the man's hat?" Shawna whispered to her mother.

"I haven't the foggiest," Claire responded.

There was something hypnotic and beguiling about this dark-eyed stranger. Shawna was desperate to ask her how she knew her father and why she was wearing that

hat, but when the fedora flew off her head, she scurried to retrieve it and instead of returning to the gravesite, she summarily disappeared. Shawna was beyond disappointed; she was crestfallen. The identity of this woman was an intriguing mystery, and Shawna felt positively compelled to solve it, no matter how long it took.

The day after the funeral, Claire began sorting through her late husband's clothing. Aghast, Shawna asked, "He's only been dead a few days and you're cleaning out his closet? How can you be so insensitive?"

"Charities need clothing, and your father had excellent taste. He owned dozens of designer suits."

"I'm sure some homeless guy will look great in them," she said with a sneer.

"He'll be the toast of Skid Row."

The days, weeks, and months passed with agonizing slowness. Numbing inertia threatened to paralyze Shawna's life. Nothing was as joyful as it would've been if her father had been there to share it with her. On several occasions, she thought she spotted the mysterious woman in the fedora. She would breathlessly chase after her only to discover that it was someone else entirely. Shawna continued to wonder what her father felt for this stranger in the felt hat.

Seven years after her father exited from the earth, Shawna came face-to-face with her first glimmer of genuine happiness. Now a junior at an Ivy League university, she met a sophomore named Jonathan Lamp and fell passionately, obsessively in love. Like her father, he was extremely tall and lanky, but *unlike* him, Jonathan Lamp had a tremendous zest for living. Shawna fell for his substantial intellect, insatiable libido, and dedication to all things cognitive. With psychology his major, Jonathan was constantly analyzing situations, making judgment calls, and drawing logical conclusions. Shawna, a neuroscience major, looked at life through a scientist's eyes. She understood that her profound bliss was a result of the dopamine bursting from the nucleus accumbens in her basal forebrain.

After four idyllic months exploring each other's minds and bodies, after sharing their short-term goals and long-term dreams, Jonathan began to grow distant. For a young man with so much vitality, he became passive, lifeless. His personality took on the qualities of a damp sponge. In the middle of a mediocre Mexican dinner at Pappasito's Cantina (the chicken was rubbery and the chimichangas too cheesy), Jonathan worked up the courage to admit he fell for a political science major named Tallulah Light. "She's Light and I'm Lamp," he explained. "There's so much electricity between us that we could ignite New England."

"Jonathan, it's only a matter of time before there'll be a blackout. A power outage of colossal proportion."

"Don't be dramatic."

"I'm a scientist," she stated. "I deal in logic."

"You cannot predict a blackout of love," he said. "You haven't even *met* her."

"But *I'm* the one you love, Jonathan, and the feeling is mutual."

"Do you love *me* or the *idea* of me?" he asked. "I think you're in love with the idea."

"No. I'm in love with the *person*, not the idea. If it were my idea, you'd be two inches shorter and less analytical," she stated.

"Please keep your voice down." He hovered forward, leaning over the table, acutely aware of the nearby diners. A woman in a leopard coat grimaced. A man with a comb-over gawked. A debutante with creamy skin and crooked teeth smiled in a commiserating way that suggested she was glad to be witnessing someone *else's* misery.

"I'm sure you'll meet another guy. You're a really great girl with all that red hair." Her thick mane was occasionally unmanageable, and Shawna wondered if that was the underlying reason for the breakup: hair upheaval. "What kind of hair does Tallulah Light have?" she asked with trepidation.

"Dark," he said. "Shoulder length. Soft and silky like a dog's coat after a bath."

"I *love* a dog's coat after a bath," Shawna confessed with deep sadness.

"Chin up," Jonathan said. Those were his parting words. He tossed two twenties on the table then briskly stood up and fled.

The next few days were spent sobbing, sniveling, and sipping various concoctions made with cranberry juice, ice cream, and Courvoisier. Shawna tried vacuuming away her anguish, but all that did was give her an impeccably clean carpet. She tried pillow punching, but all that did was strengthen the muscles in her left wrist. Desperate, distraught, and momentarily deranged, she called her mother for emotional support.

"There are many, many fish in the sea," Claire reminded her daughter, "but very few you can count on to swim home to you every night."

"So, you think I should try to win him back?"

"You can't *win* someone, darling," Claire explained. "He's not a stuffed animal at a county fair. I wish I could help you with your heartbreak, but I don't give advice on the subject. My husband chose *death* over me, remember?"

"Yes, I recall."

"I feel guilty that I didn't give you an older sister to confide in," Claire said.

"That would've been nice."

"Or an aunt."

"Right."

"Or a female cousin."

"I appreciate your guilt," Shawna said.

"My guilt won't last very long," she explained, "so you'll have to find someone else to pour your heart out to, someone who could impart a bit of much-needed wisdom. Is there a neighbor?"

"Not really," Shawna said.

"A professor perhaps?"

"No."

"A nearby nun?"

"I have to hang up now, Mother."

Night after sleepless night, Shawna tried to think of some solution, even a temporary one. Five days into her abandonment, she devised what she thought would be an interesting plan. It wouldn't be foolproof, but it would be interesting.

She studied Tallulah Light from afar, her sleek sable-brown hair framing a sculpted face—sea-green eyes, perfect little nose, tomato-red lips, smooth olive skin.

Then there was the wardrobe. Every single day, Tallulah dressed in some shade of blue—baby blue, cobalt blue, cornflower, royal, cerulean, steel, teal, midnight.

Like a warrior heading into battle, Shawna marched six blocks to Hair & Now under a sky swirling with dark, ominous clouds. A light drizzle turned into a deluge as the male stylist worked on Shawna with intense concentration. Two hours later, the rain had subsided, and Shawna left the salon. She purchased a tomato-red lipstick, then she picked up a pair of contact lenses that changed her eye color from light brown to sea green. Following that, she headed to a tanning salon and booked ten sessions. She finished the day by shopping for a new wardrobe, every article of clothing some shade of blue.

She decided the right time to reveal herself to Jonathan was immediately after his Friday morning class in schizoaffective disorders. In her double-breasted, cornflower-blue jacket with its crisp white collar, she leaned against the beige wall in the hallway. When the class ended, the students dispersed and Jonathan trotted down the corridor. Shawna scurried to catch up to him. "Jonathan!" she called out.

He quickly glanced over at her while slowing down. "Hey, Tallulah."

"My name is not Tallulah," she matter-of-factly stated.

Coming to a complete halt, Jonathan was dumbfounded. He stared at the mysterious woman as if she were a fuzzy apparition. "Wow," he mumbled. "Shawna."

"That's correct."

"You look so different. Your clothes, your hair."

"I made a few changes. Do you like the new me?"

"I do," he said.

"Thanks," Shawna responded. "I'm glad." Then she

strolled away with utter confidence, feeling his eyes still on her as though they were glued.

"I like it *very* much," he muttered to himself.

Jonathan addressed the new look immediately, *Vertigo* in reverse, delving into a detailed analysis of his ego—which he discovered was gargantuan. But his attraction to the new Shawna was so intense that none of this made the slightest difference. It took him exactly thirty minutes to call and ask her out.

Over a vegetarian dinner at the college town's most elegant restaurant, Shawna and Jonathan fell in love all over again. They studied together in the university library, read under the towering campus trees, and made Freudian love in her dorm room. (He convinced her, as Freud believed, that the sexual drive was the primary motivational force of the homosapien.) Once again, the dopamine flowed from the paraventricular nucleus of Shawna's hypothalamus, filling her with jubilance and joy.

Tallulah electrified no more.

One balmy evening at the popular seafood place Fish Frolic, Shawna and Jonathan were feasting on baked whitefish and classic Maryland crab cakes when a statuesque woman in a black fedora entered the establishment. She was seated at a table for two even though she appeared to be solo.

"What's wrong?" Jonathan asked.

"The woman who just walked in," Shawna whispered with stunned excitement. "I think I know her."

"The one in the funny hat?"

"Right."

"Do you want to say hello?"

"I have to," Shawna said as she stood up. Her hands were shaking ever so slightly and her heart pounded with anticipation.

The mystery woman removed the hat from her head. Her wavy black hair (with flecks of gray) fell past her shoulders; it seemed soft and silky as a dog's coat after a bath. She was dressed stylishly in a black silk shirt, black knit blazer and gray ankle pants.

Shawna clumsily weaved her way through a gauntlet of tables, chairs, patrons heading to the loo and servers carrying enormous platters of food. "Excuse me," she said when she finally arrived at the table. "I hate to be a bother, but I think I recognize you."

"Oh?" the woman asked defensively. She seemed annoyed by the disturbance, assaulted almost, as if Shawna had burst her bubble of seclusion.

"About ten years ago, did you attend the funeral of Charles Deardorf? He was my father."

Suddenly appearing to relax, the woman gazed into Shawna's searching green eyes. "Mon Dieu," she muttered. "Charley Deardorf. Please take a seat."

With abundant anticipation, Shawna sat down across from the femme fatale. "So it *was* you."

"Indeed. My name is Althea. Althea Iris Fawning."

"What a lovely name," Shawna said, extending her hand. "I'm Shawna Rochelle Deardorf. I've been hoping to run into you."

"Have you been searching for me all these years, Shawna Rochelle?"

"In a bizarre way I *have*," she said.

"My goodness." Althea appeared to enjoy being the object of attention.

"You see, I don't think my parents loved each other, and I was convinced my father was involved with someone else. I always imagined clandestine liaisons in secluded cabins and lingering rendezvous in romantic hideaways. Then when I saw you at the funeral, I couldn't help wondering if you were the love of my father's life."

"The love of his life," Althea repeated softly. She took a deep, troubled breath, her eyes wide and unblinking. "No. I was not the love of sweet Charley's life."

Disappointment set into Shawna's face. "Then how did you know him?"

"I was a clinical psychologist," she explained. "Your father was in session with me for a good number of years."

"I see." Shawna saw, but not nearly enough. The need to know more was unmistakable in her eyes. "Was there someone else he loved?"

Althea took her time. The only reason she even *considered* divulging details about her ex-client was that he was deceased, and his daughter seemed desperate to discover the truth about the father she cherished. "There *was* another individual," Althea said in a hushed voice. "Someone your father loved very deeply."

Shawna's face lit up. "There was?"

"Yes." Again she hesitated, falling back into her thoughts, trying to recall details, eyes completely closed. After a few moments, those eyes bolted open. "He was an Oxford-educated Englishman who worked with oceanic animals."

For more than a moment, Shawna was silent and confused. "He?"

Althea nodded. "A prominent marine mammologist

who perished during a shark attack off the coast of Nova Scotia. Gruesome."

For another moment, Shawna was silent and confused. Then a fresh-faced waitress in taupe appeared at the table with a glowing smile and two menus. "My name is Fedora and I'll be your server this evening."

"Your name is Fedora?" Shawna asked with astonishment.

"Fedora Twine, and I'd like to tell you about tonight's specials. May I?"

"By all means," Althea said, admiring Fedora's aquiline nose, fleshy body, and uncommonly long, luxurious lashes.

"We have a slow-baked Faroe Island salmon. The Faroes are an archipelago of eighteen small volcanic islands between Iceland and Norway in the North Atlantic Ocean. Because of its picturesque cliffs and valleys, it's a destination for bird-watchers and true nature lovers. Tourist season is July and August, but if you want to avoid the crowds, I'd suggest visiting in late May or early June. We also have an Ecuadorian cazuela de mariscos: a crustacean stew made with tomatoes, peppers, cumin, sage leaf, and other enticing spices to satisfy the palate. Ecuador, of course, straddles the equator on the west coast of South America. When visiting, you'll obviously want to explore the fierce Amazon jungle, but please don't forget the wildlife-rich Galapagos Islands, agreed?"

"Uh, OK, agreed," Shawna said, her head spinning. She was drowning in the news that her beloved father lived a completely separate life from the one he'd lived with his wife and daughter. How did he meet this man? Where did he find time to spend with this oceanographer?

Was he planning to tell her when she got older? Was her mother aware of this liaison?

"And finally," Fedora continued, "we offer a Nova Scotia deep-water shark steak. Almost completely surrounded by water, the province of Nova Scotia is a truly remarkable region with– "

"We know about Nova Scotia," Shawna interrupted. "A Nova Scotia shark mercilessly killed the love of my father's life."

Fedora was taken aback. "I'm sure it's not the same one," she quietly said.

Althea gazed at her young server. "You are an enchanting creature of the sea," she told her. "Do you know that?"

"What a fascinating thing to say," Fedora replied. "I always believed we as a species originated from the depths of our vast oceans."

"I should return to where *I* originated," Shawna said. "A table in the rear of the restaurant. I just felt compelled to stop by."

"Take my card, my dear," Althea reached into her large, faux leather tote.

"You may have questions later, beaucoup de questions, and you'll have a hell of a time tracking me down because I choose to be an unlisted woman."

"Thank you," Shawna said, clutching the card.

"By the way, how did you recognize me? The violet eyes? Ruby red lips?"

"Frankly, it was the fedora."

"Ah, le chapeau. Believe it or not, this very fedora was a gift from your father. I admired it on his head, and he insisted I have it."

"This was Daddy's actual fedora?"

"Mais oui. Do you know how much I'd like you to have it?"

"Very much?" she asked.

"Very much indeed."

"Thank you, Althea," Shawna gushed, eagerly reaching for the hat.

"But I can't part with it. I'm sorry."

Flummoxed, Shawna stood up, glanced quizzically at Fedora, then ambled back to Jonathan.

"Was she who you thought she was?" Jonathan asked.

"She was the woman I recognized, but she wasn't the woman I thought she was," Shawna sadly said.

Sometime between her crab cake entrée and pecan-crusted key lime pie dessert, without understanding precisely why, Shawna decided to let her hair grow back to its natural color and lose the green-tinted contact lenses. Then she swiped her palm across her mouth, forever erasing any hint of tomato-red lipstick.

Under a luminous half-moon, Jonathan locked arms with Shawna and they walked seven blocks to the car. Neither spoke very much until Jonathan stopped in his tracks, reached into his jacket pocket, and took out a small box. He presented it to Shawna, who immediately opened it to find a shimmering rose quartz engagement ring.

"Will you be my bride?" Jonathan asked as he bent down on one knee.

"This is a psychogenic shock," Shawna blurted out. "My blood vessels might be dilating and it's possible I'll pass out."

"I had a feeling you'd be surprised."

"Please stand up, Jonathan. And tuck your shirt in."

The wannabe groom followed instructions. "I'm *beyond* surprised," Shawna admitted. "This is so out of the blue that it's not even a color."

"I've been thinking a lot about settling down, and I don't want to do it with anyone except you."

"Me *Shawna*? Or the me who looks like Tallulah Light?"

Jonathan became tongue-tied. He was so taken aback that he didn't know how to respond.

"The fact that you hesitated proves we have a serious problem," she stated.

"I'm convinced we can solve any problem together as man and wife," he said.

"You mean woman and husband?"

"Sure, whatever. Queen and servant, if you want."

"Well," Shawna said, "I'd love to give you an answer right now, but I can't."

"Why not?" Jonathan asked, his jaw tightening.

"Because I might not love you as much as I thought I did. And you might not love me as much as you think you do."

"Why do you say that?" he asked.

"Because I went to extreme, ridiculous lengths to win you back. I virtually became somebody else."

"I knew exactly what you were doing and I felt sorry for you."

"I don't want your pity, Jonathan. I want someone to respect me," Shawna said. "Look, I realize I'm not entirely innocent. I fell for the first person who paid attention to me, and that was *you*. But I need to experience more life. I feel like I've just been born."

"Don't be silly. You're one year older than me."

"Then that means you're still in the womb," she told him. "Chin up, beloved sweetheart." Those were her parting words before strutting toward the twinkling lights in the distance.

When Shawna arrived home, she carefully placed the business card of Althea Iris Fawning on her night table, detecting a subtle, delectable floral scent emanating from it.

As she tried to fall asleep that night, she focused on the fascinating eccentricities of her new acquaintance. Shawna's body, head to toe, was warmed by the woman's image as if a pilot light had been lit deep inside her. The hypothalamic region of her brain was fully activated. Electric. Alive. Her pulse was racing.

She didn't know if she'd ever see the psychologist again, but she was certain there would be other Altheas. There would be women and men and places to visit and lessons to learn and an entire world to experience. And she would experience it as Shawna Deardorf with thick red hair, big chocolate eyes, and a wardrobe that had nothing to do with the color blue.

Looking for Last Year

The moment Emily Foster stepped into Fritz's West Side Dry Cleaning on 79th Street and Columbus Avenue, she knew something was different about the place. With its gray concrete floor and burgundy brick walls, the store was usually so dark that it was difficult to read a laundry ticket, but on this particular Monday morning Emily was hit with a blaze of light shooting from behind the counter. An unfamiliar giant stood six feet four inches tall with a shock of wavy hair so blond it seemed neon. Remarkably, the man's head illuminated the establishment from floor to ceiling.

Momentarily flummoxed, Emily frantically tried to put a few words together while admiring the man's aquamarine eyes that literally sparkled. His face was so exquisite, so architecturally perfect, that it deserved to be carved into the side of a mountain. "I'm here to drop off these, uh..."

"Clothes?' he inquired.

"Right. Clothes," she replied. Her heart was thumping so powerfully that she was afraid her blouse might be moving. "I've never seen you here."

"I'm helping out for a few weeks," he responded with a slight accent. "Then I go back to Finland."

"Ah, Finland," she said with affection.

"You've been there?" he excitedly asked.

"Not exactly," she admitted, instantly realizing how ridiculous that sounded. Either she'd *been* to Finland or she *hadn't*; there was no in between. "But I've seen so many pictures of the fjords that I feel like they're my second home."

"Most of the fjords are in Norway, but we do have one in Finland."

"Of course," she said. "Norway. Fjords." She desperately needed to change the subject. "Where's Fritz? Or his wife?" she asked, as if the German owners of the establishment were close pals who invited her over for schweinebraten once a month.

"They'll be in later this morning."

"I see." Emily shyly patted her hair and then wiped an imaginary piece of lint from the sleeve of her camel-hair coat. "What brought you to America?"

"An internship," he said with a touch of embarrassment. "Yah, still a student at twenty-two."

"I'm still paying off my student loan at twenty-seven," she said although she was twenty-eight, as if chopping one year off her age would make a difference in the way the Adonis regarded her. "I *grew up* in New York, so if you need someone to show you around the city, it would be my pleasure." She was aghast that these words emerged from her mouth no more than ninety seconds after meeting the man. Never had she been so forward. She'd certainly never offered her services as a Manhattan tour guide before.

"You would show me around?" he asked with surprise.

"Absolutely," she replied. "I'm Emily, by the way."

"My name is Mathias."

"Mathias. Beautiful." *Say it loud and it's music playing*, she thought to herself. *Say it soft and it's almost like praying.* "Mathias."

"It's fairly common in Finland," he explained. "Norway, too."

Emily nodded, thinking there was *nothing* common about this man. She accepted the fact that what she felt was lust, pure and simple, and she hadn't felt anything like it in two-and-a-quarter years.

"Let me give you a ticket," Mathias said, referring to the heap of clothing Emily had tossed on the counter. "Four blouses, one jacket. Is Friday after five all right?"

"Just fine."

"Last name?"

"Foster," she told him.

"Foster, Emily." He wrote it down and then handed her the ticket, which she gingerly placed in her bag. "If you're free tonight, we can meet in front at six," he suggested. "For the tour."

"Yes, absolutely!" she responded with enthusiasm. "Six is perfect."

Emily didn't want to leave, but there was no rational reason for her to stay.

She took her time moseying to the door and then shot Mathias a quick, over-the-shoulder smile before exiting the premises.

The once-engaged twenty-eight-year-old was familiar with the longings and letdowns of love. Luckily, the true colors of her ex-fiancé surfaced a week before the wedding, and Emily had the permanent scars to prove it. The phantom limb of that doomed relationship still hurt, and the experience taught her to proceed with caution.

Still, the exhilaration of meeting Mathias was overwhelming; it left her feeling giddy, jubilant. She would've done a cartwheel if she knew how. She would've tossed her hat in the air if she'd been wearing one. She actually had to hold herself back from throwing her arms open and hugging several passersby. Never before had elation taken over so powerfully inside her.

The streets of Manhattan's Upper West Side were bustling with young mothers pushing baby carriages, muscular men marching to and from the gym, and ambitious thirtysomethings rushing to corporate offices, mobile phones glued to their ears. Ordinarily, Emily would've caught a bus or the subway to get to midtown, but she had so much euphoric energy that she decided to walk. Fall had officially arrived, and the chill in the October air was invigorating.

Interrupting the joyful stroll, a troubling thought entered Emily's hyperactive mind: Where would she take Mathias on this tour of New York? Though her knowledge of the city was thorough, her background as a tour guide was nil. She didn't know where to begin or where to end, and she certainly didn't know what would make up the middle.

There were the quintessential landmarks like Madison Square Garden and the Empire State Building. There were restaurants, museums, promenades, and parks. Did he want to catch a Broadway show? Visit the Guggenheim? Would he be interested in the skating rink at Rockefeller Center? The Statue of Liberty? The options were endless, and Emily's head felt like it was on the verge of exploding. She decided to think about the tour later in the day, after she thoroughly and completely calmed down.

Emily arrived at her destination just a few minutes later than usual. Inside the lobby of the towering office building, she scurried to the snack bar and ordered a cup of coffee. Then she grabbed a banana and a newspaper. After turning down the offer of a paper bag, she carried the items in her hands and hurried to the one of the elevators that was jam-packed and ready for take-off.

An outgoing young man in a blue blazer said, "We can fit one more." This invitation elicited an audible groan from some impatient person in the back of the car, but that didn't stop Emily from squeezing in. "Thank you," she whispered to the guy in blue.

After opening on two, four, five, and six, the imposing silver doors parted on floor number seven, and Emily exited swiftly. A doe-eyed woman carrying an armful of file folders was walking toward her. "Emily," the woman said with bewilderment.

"Hello, Lisa," she replied without stopping to chat. She strolled down the carpeted corridor and entered a spacious room filled with rows of identical cubicles.

After planting herself in the first cubicle of the third row, she removed her coat and hung it in the nearby closet. Then she returned to her desk and began to peel her banana.

Carrying coffee in a large ceramic mug, Jocelyn Meade was heading to a morning meeting of department heads. With necklaces glittering and bracelets jiggling, she stopped in her tracks a few feet from Emily's cubicle. "Emily," she said, her eyes wide with surprise. "I can't believe it. What are you doing here?"

"Excuse me?"

Just then, Jocelyn noticed her department head,

Kendall Herzog, marching down the hallway, swathed in pearls and pink cashmere, with the big sprayed hair of a television anchorwoman. "Kendall," she called out, "Look who's here."

Kendall approached, her manner haughty, supercilious. "My God, Emily Foster," she blurted out with disbelief.

"Why is everyone so shocked to see me?" Emily asked.

"What, may I ask, are you doing in this office?" Kendall inquired with the warmth of a glacier.

"I'm here to work, obviously," Emily stated with conviction.

"Is this some kind of joke?" Kendall asked, glancing around for a hidden camera.

"What kind of joke? I don't understand."

Kendall took a deep, anguished breath. "You are no longer employed here, young lady," she brusquely declared. "You were let go."

In a prolonged moment of silence, Emily allowed this startling information to sink in. "Let go," she muttered. "Did someone neglect to tell me this?"

"You *were* told," Kendall assured her. "In my office."

"And when exactly was this?"

"It's been a year or so," Jocelyn interjected in a suddenly concerned tone of voice.

"A year or so," Emily repeated. She looked ashen.

"We had to cut back on staff," Kendall explained. "Don't you remember?"

Emily stared vacantly at the two women standing above her. "Cut back on staff. Now I remember." She didn't remember, and she was beginning to feel dizzy.

"You need to pick up your belongings and leave,"

Kendall ordered quietly but sternly, impervious to Emily's embarrassment. "Right now, before I call security."

"You don't need to call security," Jocelyn said to her irritable colleague, who reacted with an expression of cold loathing.

"Why don't you escort Emily to the lobby?" Kendall ordered.

"Of course," Jocelyn replied.

Positively mortified, Emily reached for her handbag and newspaper, opting to leave the banana and coffee behind. "I guess I lost track of time," she explained as she struggled up from her chair. She lumbered to the closet and yanked her coat off its hanger.

"Your hair's longer," Jocelyn remarked. "I like it."

"Thanks," Emily mumbled.

"Mine's become unmanageable," Jocelyn confessed, running a hand through her frizzy blonde locks as her bracelets jiggled.

"Must you wear such noisy jewelry?" Kendall snapped. "They induce migraines." She glanced sharply at Emily before strolling purposefully down the hall.

In tense silence, Emily buttoned her camel-hair coat from top to bottom and discovered, to her embarrassment, that one of the brass buttons was missing. As calmly as she could, she marched down the carpeted corridor as if walking the plank in purgatory. Jocelyn followed closely behind. Then, seven floors down, they stepped onto the marble floor of the massive lobby. "Well, take care of yourself," Jocelyn said.

"Yes," Emily meekly replied. "I will."

And that was that.

Certain that her humiliation was obvious, Emily

avoided eye contact with every one of the thousands of New Yorkers swarming the sidewalks. She felt like she had just endured a severe public flogging in the town square. Trembling, she wandered north on Madison Avenue and then veered over to Sixth, wondering if her mind was deteriorating or merely playing tricks on her. Tricks had been played before, but they were fairly benign. Showing up to a place of employment where she hadn't been employed for a year was anything *but* benign. For the moment, however, she decided to chalk it up to a simple memory lapse, like forgetting to take out the trash.

Near Columbus Circle, Emily bumped into a young woman carrying a yoga mat under her arm, causing the mat to fall to the ground. She apologized profusely, but the woman said nothing, choosing to pretend it didn't happen. Realizing she hadn't taken a single sip of the coffee or bite of the banana she'd left behind, Emily searched for a place to sit down and have a proper breakfast. An empty table at an outdoor café caught her eye, and she grabbed it.

A swarthy young server named Sergio appeared with a menu. "Would you like coffee?" he asked.

"Yes, please," she said.

As soon as Sergio walked away, Emily noticed a miniature bottle of ketchup on the table. Thinking it was ridiculously cute, she slipped the tiny bottle into her handbag. When Sergio returned with a steaming cup of coffee, Emily was struck with fear, certain he would accuse her of stealing. "Would you like anything else?" he inquired.

At first, she thought Sergio was asking whether she'd like anything else to sneak into her purse. Then she realized she was being paranoid, and the waiter was just doing his job. "Uh, yes," she said. "Can I have two scrambled eggs with bacon and fruit? And sourdough toast with jam."

"Of course," he said with a smile as Emily breathed a sigh of relief, truly pleased that she avoided arrest and a potential night in the slammer.

A middle-aged man in a solid-blue shirt took a seat two tables away. He lit a cigarette, opened his laptop, and began working. Sergio greeted this new customer and handed him a menu.

It wasn't long before Emily's breakfast was delivered, and she began to eat her eggs. That's when she noticed the man's shirt wasn't blue at all. It was magenta. She wondered how she could have been so mistaken.

After she finished her tasty meal, Sergio came by to remove her plate. "Excuse me," she whispered to him. He leaned down to listen. "What color would you say that man's shirt is?" she asked, breathing in his delicious musky scent.

The server glanced at his other outdoor customer. "I'd say bright pink," he whispered back.

"Thanks," she said. "That's what I thought."

"Would you like more coffee?" he asked, his voice back to normal volume.

"No thanks. I'll just take the check."

After paying the bill and leaving a huge tip, Emily realized she had hours to kill. She contemplated ambling through the Upper West Side or perusing the crowded shelves of a bookstore but in the end decided to head home for a nap and a Xanax.

On the road were Mack trucks, buses, and motorbikes,

but not a single available taxi. Frustrated, she walked two blocks north. Finally a cab pulled up and Emily jumped in.

Between bumper-to-bumper traffic and uncooperative stoplights, the ride was exceptionally slow, but Emily didn't mind. She focused on the magnificent image of her shining knight looming in her head.

The driver pulled up to an old brick building on West 84th Street. Emily handed him a generous tip, entered the building, and took the elevator to the fifth floor. Then she dashed to apartment 5-J.

When she attempted to unlock the door, her key didn't slide in as she expected. She tinkered with it, and a few seconds later the door swung open. A shaggy-haired guy in an untucked flannel shirt and well-worn blue jeans stood there, barefoot. "I *thought* I heard someone," Luke said.

"That was me," Emily announced as she entered the small, cluttered apartment that smelled of cinnamon potpourri.

"What's going on?" Luke asked, perplexed.

"You have a girlfriend," she stated with certainty.

He seemed surprised. "How'd you know that?"

"It wasn't *you* who bought the potpourri, Luke."

"You should be a detective."

"So, tell me," she said, abruptly changing the subject, "if you were an out-of-towner visiting New York, what are the three tourist spots you'd want to visit?" Luke peered at Emily, bewildered. "Tell me the top three sights you'd want to see in the city."

"What is going on with you?" he asked. "Don't you think it's a little strange to suddenly show up here?"

She hesitated. "Luke, please tell me what's strange

about it."

"It's strange because you moved out last year," he explained. "You told me you couldn't stand me anymore, remember?"

For a long moment she stared at him in open-mouthed disbelief. She seemed to be slipping out of her life. Was she living in some other dimension, she wondered? Some alternate universe? Obviously, something was terribly wrong, wrong enough to warrant checking into a mental health facility. But she refused to risk her date with Mathias; the evaluation would have to be put on hold for twenty-four hours. "All right," she said, attempting to remain calm, "if I moved out, where do I live now?"

"You found an apartment off Columbus," Luke informed her. "In the upper 80s, I think. I wasn't invited to the housewarming, so I can't provide any details."

"I'm sorry," she quietly said.

"Did you really think you still lived here?" he asked with concern.

"I wasn't thinking," she said, woefully wobbly.

"Well, I think you need to see someone, Em. Right away."

"I'm seeing someone at six," she told him.

"That's good," he said with compassion. "Is there anything I can do?" She felt helpless and pitiful, like an impoverished mother being visited by a well-meaning but phony government official. "It's all coming back," she said, stepping over a stack of magazines and an empty pizza carton on her way to the kitchen. "I was making dinner, baked Rigoletto with eggplant, and you were with that blonde across the hall. Eva."

"I think you mean rigatoni. And her name was Ava. She moved out."

"Pity," Emily said. "I see you haven't done the dishes since I left."

"It's on my agenda for the fall," Luke responded with a smirk. "Are you all right?"

"You said I found an apartment off Columbus?" she asked, her breathing unsteady. "In the upper 80s?"

"That's right."

She wished an oxygen mask would drop from the ceiling. "Could you do me a big favor, Luke? Could you try to remember the exact address?"

The sun, surrounded by billows of soft pink clouds, was beginning to sink into the horizon, and the tops of skyscrapers appeared golden in the fading light. The temperature had fallen almost twenty degrees, and the wind had become fierce. Only two blocks from Fritz's West Side Dry Cleaning, Emily's heart, fueled by equal parts promise and trepidation, began to race. She knew the moment she'd see Mathias, the problems of her bizarre and unusual day would melt away.

When she stepped onto 79th Street, she was hoping to spot the Nordic god halfway down the block, towering above everybody else. But the street was uncommonly crowded, and its inhabitants were choking on the fumes of taxi cabs, trucks, and clouds of hissing steam coming from the underground subway.

Walking against the powerful wind, Emily felt like a soldier heading into battle. Several pedestrians accidentally bumped into her, and one obnoxious six-year-old boy deliberately stepped on her foot. It took almost five exhausting minutes to reach her destination and an additional thirty seconds to pull the heavy glass door open. The slender, middle-aged owner of the establishment was standing behind the counter. "Can I help you?" Fritz asked in a heavy German accent even though he'd been living in New York for thirty-five years. "Yes," Emily responded. "I'm here to see Mathias."

Fritz peered at her with blank bewilderment. "I don't know."

"The tall Norwegian guy who helped me this morning."

"Another dry cleaner."

"No, no, no," she insisted. "It was right here, in this exact spot."

From behind a calm sea of plastic-covered clothing on hangers, Reinhilde appeared. "Looking for Mathias," Fritz told his wife, a woman with curved, menacing eyebrows and a hostile frown sewn into her face.

"Mathias from Finland," Emily said. "I had an encounter with him right here at the counter."

Reinhilde turned to Fritz. "Mathias," she said. "Tall."

"Right!" Emily exclaimed. "He's the one. Very tall. Like a giant."

"What you need?"

"I'm supposed to meet him here. Can you get him for me please?"

"In Helsinki," Reinhilde said.

"That's not possible. We were supposed to meet here at six."

"Helsinki," Reinhilde repeated. "Went home to Helsinki."

"That couldn't be right," Emily said, shaking her head in stubborn denial.

"Yes, is right."

"But he was here this morning," Emily asserted. "I'm not leaving until you bring him out."

"Not here," Reinhilde stated emphatically, attempting to put an end to the conversation.

"Where... is... Mathias?" Emily asked between clenched teeth.

"Leave dry cleaner now or we call police," Reinhilde threatened.

"I'm not leaving!" Emily shouted. "I need Mathias! We met here this very morning!" There was such urgency in her cry, such desperation in her voice, that Reinhilde was severely taken aback. She shot her husband a distressed look and he immediately picked up the landline next to the cash register.

"No!" Emily yelled, panicked. "No police. Put the phone down. I'll go. I'll go right now." With shaky limbs, she hobbled to the glass door. She tried to pull it toward her, but it was too heavy. Fritz saw her struggling and he hurried over to help.

Feeling as if her legs might collapse, Emily took a couple of tiny steps on the broken sidewalk, but she was so weak that she descended to the ground and huddled against the glass. Just then, a gargantuan garbage truck roared its way down the street, terrifying her. She was relieved when the sound dissipated, but the soothing quiet was interrupted by Reinhilde's bellowing voice. "Blocking entrance!" she shrieked, causing Emily to feel ambushed, as if caught smoking grass in a stairwell by an enraged high school principal. "Is verboten for you to sit here."

"Verboten," Emily muttered. "Where are we, Bergen-Belsen?" With difficulty, she managed to lift herself off the cement as Reinhilde stood her ground.

Emily staggered over to the nearest taxi. There were two lifeless human figures propped up like crash-lab dummies in the back seat, so she headed to the taxi behind it. There were three lifeless human forms in the back seat, so she headed to the taxi behind it. Thankfully the back seat was devoid of dummies, and Emily climbed in. Before saying a word to the driver, she leaned her head against the leather, realizing her life was unraveling as quickly as darkness was descending on the city.

With quivering fingers, she opened her wallet, fumbled for her driver's license, and read the address to the impatient driver. While enduring the slow and bumpy ride, Emily massaged her temples as though trying to ward off a migraine. When tears came pouring down, they were tears of fear and confusion, and she didn't fight them.

The driver dropped her off in front of a fire hydrant and pointed to a brick building that looked vaguely familiar. She gave him a decent tip and then climbed out of the cab.

Emily made it up to apartment 4-B. It took several attempts but her key finally slid into the lock, and she breathed an enormous sigh of relief. She stepped into the minimally furnished place, which was flooded with moonlight coming in from the living room window. In a comforting flash of clarity, Emily recalled that she had friends, parents, and a sister. After finding her mother's phone number in a leather-bound directory, she grabbed her cell phone and pressed the buttons.

"Mother?" she asked with trepidation.

"Emily. What's wrong?"

"Something's happening to me," she said. "My head, my brain. Strange things that I can't explain."

Within an hour, Emily's concerned mother, father, and sister were perched on the living room sofa like a row of birds atop a billboard on a cloudy day. "You begged us to let you live on your own, remember?" her mother asked.

"You thought you were well enough," her father added.

"What exactly happened today?" Renata asked.

Slowly and methodically, Emily recounted the story of her roller-coaster ride of a day beginning with the bizarre workplace incident. Then she moved on to the magic shirt that morphed from blue to pink. She continued with her awkward interaction with Luke, and finished with the Finnish god and his disappearing act at the dry cleaning shop. As her family listened with concern, Emily felt proud of herself for facing the difficult truth while holding on to what was left of her fraying sanity.

"You can't go out alone anymore," Renata instructed. "It's that simple."

"And I don't want you living by yourself," her mother stated. "You'll come home with us."

"You have to be examined by a doctor," her father said. "A neurologist."

"They'll pinpoint exactly what's wrong," Renata added. "You'll take MRIs, brain scans, all sorts of tests. It's miraculous what they can do these days."

Gradually the words became a blur as her eyelids became too heavy to remain open. Exhausted, Emily wanted nothing more than to lose herself in the safety of a deep, peaceful sleep where her dreams could transport her to a pleasant place, where everything was clear and comprehensible.

"We'll see you through this, honey," her mother assured her.

"We're right here," Renata added.

There was nothing for Emily to do but believe them.

Familiar Eyes

Phoenix, Arizona held no fascination for corporate attorney Rachel Copeland, but it was the city closest to a tiny town called Morena (population: 1,480) that was, according to public records, the place of residence of a Mr. Seth Turner. Now a San Francisco resident, Rachel had grown up in Tucson, Arizona, but her family had dispersed all over the country—Santa Fe, Atlanta, San Diego—so she hadn't been to her home state in almost a decade. She knew that she couldn't wipe out her distant past by clicking *delete,* but she hoped a short trip might help her close one particular chapter, a dark and traumatic one. On a bizarre impulse, she booked a seat on a flight to Phoenix for later that very day.

The two-hour flight was uneventful except for the crass bonehead who refused to mind his own business in business class. Luckily, experience had taught Rachel how to handle married men with roving eyes and index fingers. She leaned over and whispered into his large fuzzy ear: "I think you're hot, but my genital herpes just became active after six months of lying dormant and I'd feel so guilty infecting you."

After landing in Phoenix, Rachel rented one of the clunky white sedans that stood on the parking lot of the rental agency. She'd forgotten how hot, humid, sticky, airless, sweltering, and oppressive Arizona could be, even in February. The temperature was soaring toward three digits and she was dressed for a cool autumn evening. She was surprised the car itself wasn't sweating.

Dusk was beginning to darken the day as Rachel weaved her way through the mild traffic on the freeway. An eerie suspense hung in the air, along with a stale odor of smoke and liquor from the faux leather seats of the rental. The distinct possibility that this reluctant voyage, this spur-of-the-moment excursion, might amount to nothing didn't bother her. The scenario had been in her head for so long that it was time to either bring it to vivid life or drop it once and for all into the garbage dump of her subconscious mind. She was on a mission, but she couldn't even guess at the outcome.

Just past six-thirty p.m., Rachel zoomed into the small town of Morena with its abandoned buildings and drug traffickers lurking in dark, menacing alleys. A couple of bored young hookers stood on a street corner; business wasn't brisk. In the drab, depressing gray landscape, it seemed as if even the *trees* had given up on any kind of fulfilling life; their withering brown leaves hung lifelessly, waiting to fall from their branches and disintegrate. Thankfully, a bright crescent moon hung in the sky like a slice of melon, its shimmering silver glow radiating something that resembled hope.

Torrence Boulevard was the center of the community, the heartbeat of this hideous place, and the location of a dive bar called Cy's. In a strip mall that housed a dilapidated convenience store and a coin-operated Laundromat, Cy's stood under a rusty tin roof and a red neon sign that failed to light up the apostrophe. Rachel pulled into a diagonal spot near the bar's entrance.

Inside, the dimly lit pub consisted of dark wood-paneled walls, burgundy leather booths, and a pool table that had seen better nights. The happy hour crowd numbered a couple of dozen, but none seemed particularly happy. Predominantly male and blue-collar, they were kicking back after an arduous day of hard labor on a nearby construction site. The guys smoked like city buses and guzzled beer like college students at a keg party. The few women present had likely never heard of *Glamour* or *Vogue*, and it was a sure bet that *nobody* was a season-ticket holder to the Phoenix Symphony. This was the town's gathering place, but nothing linked these patrons except their dead-end lives.

Rachel hesitantly approached the bar and ordered a glass of white wine from the lanky bartender. "Four bucks," he said.

She handed him a ten. "Keep it," she told him as she sat down on a rickety barstool. He responded with a genuine, appreciative smile.

A big-boned, platinum blonde with a gigantic slab of a bosom eyed Rachel suspiciously; she didn't appreciate the classy competition. A brawny guy in a black T-shirt flashed Rachel a seductive grin as he approached her. "Howdy," he said.

"Is this the town's most popular hangout?" she asked.

"Town's *only* hangout," he chuckled, glancing at Rachel's long legs that sprouted from her expensive skirt. Closing in on forty, she appeared ten years younger.

Rachel didn't have trouble attracting men. The trouble arose when they wanted more than a superficial fling; she had a minor problem with commitment.

Rachel surveyed the patrons of the bar coolly, and

then her emerald-green eyes fell upon a man sitting alone at a booth in the back. An inexplicable sensation drew her to him; she wondered if he was Seth Turner. "Excuse me," she said to the brawny man, her brawny fan who registered disappointment when she inched away from him.

Stepping slowly on the concrete floor, her designer heels clacking normally as if her life wasn't about to radically change, she waded through the shadows and light, unwavering in her resolve to face this man one final time.

If he was the man she suspected he was.

If he was the man she hadn't seen in more than thirty years.

If she wasn't about to make a complete and utter fool of herself.

The air seemed to change as she approached the rear of the room, as though she'd reached the top of Mount Everest. She couldn't seem to catch her breath. Her vision was blurring. "Mind if I sit here a minute?" she asked the stranger slumped against the burgundy leather. With a cigarette dangling from his lips and smoke crawling up his face, he clutched a bottle of Bud Light like it was his lifeline.

Gradually, his eyes wandered from her legs to her waist to her chest and finally to her face. "It's a public place," he said.

"Yeah, I had a feeling it wasn't a private club with a huge annual fee," she remarked as she descended onto the squeaky booth patched every few inches with duct tape. The long-haired loner, coarse, disheveled, in desperate need of a shave not to mention a shower, took his time to take her in, unsure what to make of this well-dressed, articulate woman sitting across from him.

"My name is Nancy," Rachel told him, breathing with difficulty.

"Nancy," he mumbled.

"And you are...?" she inquired.

"A guy having a beer."

"OK. And I'm a gal with a glass of wine."

"Good for you."

"I'm not bragging. Just making conversation with some anonymous dude," Rachel explained. "Not much of a talker, huh?"

"Not as a general rule," he said, putting out his cigarette.

"Well, give me two minutes, then I'll leave you alone."

"Seth," he quietly said. "Name's Seth."

A shiver jolted her. Then she fell silent. She tried her best to keep her hands on her lap instead of allowing them to find their way to Seth's neck for the purpose of strangulation. *Of course* it was Seth Turner; how could she have questioned it? Years of drinking had stripped him of his youthful beauty, but he was still Seth Turner. The body was bloated, the face creased and doughy, but the prominent cleft still gave the chin a special distinction. She saw him so clearly now, so unmistakably, that she had to look away, fearing she might pass out. It seemed the decades had only exacerbated Rachel's hostility against this man. After taking a very slow and deep breath, she asked, "Did you know that Seth was supposedly the third son of Adam and Eve?"

"I'm not into all that Bible crap."

"Why doesn't that surprise me?" she whispered to

herself. "Hey, is this place known for any particular cocktail?" she asked, recalling the glass of iced tea he had once insisted she drink, the tea that tasted like medicine.

"Stale beer," he said. The exuberant bravado that once dazzled, the golden appeal that once glowed, had decayed into a faded-yellow façade, almost unrecognizable. The spirit had been squeezed from him the way water is squeezed from a sponge. Resigned to the fact that his luck would never change, this was what had become of the neighborhood Adonis who had poisoned, invaded, attacked, mutilated, harmed, and used Rachel's much-too-young body, destroying something deep inside her, damaging her in every conceivable way. The only positive by-product was that she became an expert at self-defense.

"What's there to do in this little town?" she asked, trying to disguise the shakiness in her voice.

"You don't live here?"

"Just passing through."

"Perfect town to pass through," he said. "Stay here, you go psychotic."

She emitted a short, nervous laugh. "Are you psychotic?"

"I was born that way," he said with a devious half-smile.

The staccato clack of a pool cue slamming a billiard ball sliced the thick barroom air. Then came the crash of the ball against the triangular rack that seemed amplified. Sweat was gathering on Rachel's forehead. She lifted one of her vibrating hands from under the table and wiped the perspiration away. She could still feel his boiling, stinging sweat dripping onto her face; it might as well have been hot wax. It might as well have been five seconds ago.

"You married?" she asked.

"Nah, you?"

"Nope."

"Kids?"

"No," she said, trying to maintain her equilibrium. "No children for me."

"Well," Seth said, "I'm too old for you."

Rachel seemed taken aback. "Excuse me?" she asked. "Did that sound like an invitation?"

"I'm too old for *anything*," he explained, leaning his head back on the hard leather surface. He seemed to be at home in this tavern, an old clinging vine growing on its very foundation. She remembered his bedroom walls plastered with posters of sci-fi flicks. She recalled how he stuffed her mouth with his fist so that she wouldn't be able to scream. But she *wouldn't* have screamed; she was too terrified to make any sound, too scared to move a muscle. Now she glanced at his weathered hand on the table, the same hand she had tasted in her mouth. She wondered how a human body could've changed so drastically. For her, the result was startling; it was difficult for her to believe her assessing eyes were telling her the truth. For Seth, it was likely a gradual metamorphosis that had more to do with decades of drinking, smoking, and wallowing in misery than anything else. Was he tormented by guilt? Had he done this to other young girls? How many? One or two? Ten? Twenty? The questions swirled in Rachel's head.

"What's a classy dame like you doing in a dive like this?" he asked. "You lead a double life?"

"That's me," she joked, "harried lawyer by day, happy hooker by night." The tattoos on his arms were new, or maybe just new to *her*. He'd sported no tattoos on that scorching summer day when she struggled to make her way home in hundred-degree heat, stopping only to throw up on Marta Lansing's front lawn.

Seth's eyes wandered to the large-bosomed blonde at the bar. "Dames around here either look like that," he said, "or her grandmother. They don't look like *you*."

"Should I take that as a compliment?" she asked.

"Take it any damn way you want."

"All right then," Rachel said. "Did you work today?"

"You're full of questions." His teeth were chipped and discolored. It was likely he hadn't seen a dentist in decades. "Nah, didn't work today," he said, still clutching his beer bottle as if he were terrified to part with it. "Or yesterday. Sometimes you get a lousy deal, you know?"

"Right," she said. "But sometimes you deal the cards yourself." She wanted to pound the man's head against the knotty pine wall until it bled, until he begged for the pulsating pain to stop, but first she had to fight the impulse to take his calloused hand and caress it with tenderness. Despite what he had done to her, despite the decades of anguish he'd caused, a familiar face from childhood was staring at her from across the table, and the connection was eerie and overwhelming. Though she tried, she couldn't help seeing the beautiful seventeen-year-old Seth had been, and she wanted nothing more than to travel back in time to change their violent story. She wondered whether it was fair to judge someone for a crime he'd committed when he was just a kid, a teenager with a touch of acne and no sense of responsibility. She wondered whether fairness even played a part at this point.

Rachel's head was spinning with rage, compassion, pity, and fear, combining like chemicals that weren't meant to mix. She was unable to make sense of it because she still felt embattled, ready to fight.

"Do we know each other?" Seth asked.

"Know each other?" she repeated quizzically, gripping her wine glass, instantly feeling a sense of panic. "I don't think so." A nervous giggle unwittingly emerged from her; where it came from she had no idea. But she realized she had spoken the truth: they *didn't* know each other. She had never met this woebegone figure with filthy fingernails, abundant self-pity, and hunched-over posture. The Seth Rachel knew was a confident young guy glistening with charisma and clean as a bar of bath soap, a neighborhood heartthrob who was neatly folded into the innocent first decade of her life. Before the attack. Now he was a decaying wreck, a failure, an outcast, the result of some serious karmic comeuppance. "Why do you sit so far in the back?" she asked.

"Nobody bothers me here," he explained.

"You don't like to be bothered?"

"Don't like people prying," he said.

Rachel wondered how many Bud Lights he had tossed back before she arrived and how many more he would buy before calling it a night. She wondered whether this was his typical nighttime activity—getting soused at the local tavern and then traipsing home alone, feeling sorry for himself. "Well," she said as she struggled up from the booth, "I've pried long enough."

"You're not prying," Seth told her. "You can stay if you want."

"Actually, I need to hit the road," she said. "It's getting

late for me."

"Suit yourself."

Rachel took one long, final look into the eyes of the half-dead man who dominated her past but would be undoubtedly absent from her future. "Goodbye," she said.

"You can stay," he said with difficulty. "If you want."

"I don't want to," she stated. Rachel felt the brutal, unmerciful loneliness Seth must feel every day of his infinitely sad, middle-aged life. "Makes us even, I guess." She remained another few moments, monitoring his blank expression. Then she headed toward the front door, stopping at the bar to hand the bartender a twenty dollar bill. "Buy that guy in the back a couple of Bud Lights, OK?"

The bartender glanced at Seth. "Turner?" he asked.

"Yes," she replied. "Turner."

Rachel wondered whether Seth was mystified. *Makes us even, I guess.* Did he give it a second thought? Did he try to figure out what she meant? She suppressed a desire to turn around and look at him one final time. She fought an even stronger urge to march over and tell him she was the ten-year-old girl he had invited into his house on that sweltering Friday afternoon so many years ago.

Rachel bolted out of the tavern, feeling Seth Turner's penetrating gaze on her until she stepped into the balmy night air. As if escaping to safety, she jumped into the rental car and immediately locked the doors. Physically exhausted, emotionally drained, she closed her eyes and leaned her head back. She could barely control her frantic breathing.

Rachel took her time. She was afraid to open her eyes, terrified that Seth might be standing there, watching her through the windshield. When she finally did open them, she was greatly relieved to see no one standing in front of the car, in the front of the bar, or anywhere.

The wetness on her face, a combination of sweat and tears, was wiped away in one fell swoop with her hands. Then, with determination, Rachel shoved the car key into the ignition. She fled from this bleak, somber town, eager to start living the next chapter of her life.

Island Envy

They met on a deserted island called Phog East, fifteen miles off the coast of New London, Rhode Island. Evan Donally's rowboat had capsized while he was fishing for a compliment, and he swam to the remote island in freezing water.

Fanny Gurk grew up with four strapping brothers in a busy fishing village practically run by her megalomaniac father. Attempting to make sense of a romance that fizzled (in addition to several other personal dramas), Fanny went fishing for logic when a powerful (though predicted) storm tossed her into subzero-temperature water and transported her to the western part of Phog East. Soaking wet and freezing cold, she washed ashore in one shoe. The fierce waves had whisked away the tartan ballet flat that had been on her left foot.

On the day they met, Evan had been exploring the island while Fanny caught up on her rest and resentment. Just as the fog was rolling in, Evan came upon a discarded barbecue and a deceased pig. With the confidence of a master chef, he began preparing his first meal in two days. After lighting the barbecue the old-fashioned way, he secured the sow onto one of the sticks that doubled as a spit.

Fanny caught a whiff of roasting pork and assumed she was dreaming. After pinching herself several times on various body parts, she followed the scent like a private investigator, step-by-step, until she came upon Evan Donally and his potential dinner.

For a moment, Evan assumed he was hallucinating. Out of the thick gray fog emerged what looked like a lovely young woman in a tattered black tunic and a single shoe. Her mane of reddish hair was wildly disheveled, sticking out in odd angles, but her fiery dark eyes seemed as clear and alert as could be. Evan was certain it was his lack of sustenance that created this quirky apparition.

"You're not real, are you?" he asked. "Of course you're not. But I hope you'll stay a while."

"I don't eat animals," she snapped. "This is a longshot, but do you happen to have a spinach soufflé simmering someplace?"

"You speak the language," he said, surprised and delighted.

"Did you think I spoke Farsi?"

"Are you human?" he asked with eager innocence.

"Is that what being on an island does to you—makes you lose your frigging mind? My name is Fanny, and I washed ashore with some other debris."

"I'm Evan," he responded, studying his guest. Beautiful in a quirky way, Fanny's face was a bit roundish and eyebrows a bit thick, but these imperfections made her infinitely more interesting that some skinny model on the cover of Cosmopolitan. "You're beautiful in a quirky way, you know that?" Evan asked.

"Your face is a bit roundish and eyebrows a bit thick, but these imperfections make you much more interesting that some skinny-ass model on the cover of Cosmo."

"Are you always this weird?" she inquired.

"Not always. I've been alone on a deserted island for a few days."

With major attitude, Fanny turned away and found a suitable patch of sand to call her own. She plopped down. "Is that a pig on the barbecue?"

"Yes," he announced. "Please don't tell me you keep kosher."

"I told you, I don't eat meat," she said. "Has your memory been reduced to rubble?"

"Very possibly. Why no meat?"

"Because the idea of it nauseates me," she explained. "I don't want to look at what became of cattle that were shot in the head with a metal bolt or cows that were dismembered alive or squealing hogs that were submerged into boiling water to loosen their hide."

"Gotcha," Evan said. He took a few steps closer to Fanny and descended to the ground, on his knees, under the influence of her sexy, bohemian charm. "Listen, it looks like we're the only ones on this island, so why don't we try to get along? We obviously got off on the wrong foot, but *you* know as well as I do that in time we'll bond. We'll become very close and wildly attracted to one another, so why don't we skip the middle part and jump to the inevitable?"

"Inevitable?" she asked.

"Passionate sex. Frenetic fornication. Right here, right now. It would be a terrific icebreaker, don't you think?"

She gazed into his big, brown, cartoon eyes. "I think you need a psychiatric evaluation by a medical professional. But feel free to toss any other ideas my way."

"Well," he said, the wheels spinning in his head, "would you mind if I borrowed one of your legs for a bit?

Kind of like taking a book out from a library?" His voice was pleading.

"Don't think so. I may want to walk at some point very soon."

"I would kiss and caress it, that's all," he explained, throbbing with desire. "Five minutes, then I'd give it back."

"I told you," she shouted, annoyed. *"I don't think so!"* Then she covered her face with her filthy hands. "You suppose anybody's searching for you?"

"The entire Coast Guard," he said. "How about you?"

"Not a soul," she replied. "Everyone I know will think I disappeared on purpose. It's not the first time I left the time zone and zip code."

"A rebel! I *like* that in a girl."

"You're an idiot. I *detest* that in a guy."

Evan took a frustrated breath. "Can you say *anything* nice?"

"Not in the next hour, bro." She peered at the vast but confining sky, the planet's glass ceiling, and emitted a sigh. "How long have you been here?"

"Two glorious days, two exquisite nights. You?"

"Three."

"What do you suppose the lesson is? There has to be a lesson when you're shipwrecked like the Skipper and Gilligan."

"And the movie star and Mary Ann? The lesson is don't try to kill yourself by sailing into a heavy storm."

The smile that seemed sewn on Evan's face collapsed. "You were trying to end it all?"

"I would've jumped off a roof but I'm deathly afraid of heights."

"Drowning in freezing water is a more appealing scenario?" he asked.

"Much."

He felt a wave of tenderness for his island mate. "Was your life really that lousy?"

"No, it was worse," Fanny said, staring gloomily at the sea that kept her alive instead of drowning her as it was supposed to do. "Here's the *real* reason nobody's searching for me: Nobody will miss me. I haven't made any lasting impression on anybody I've met in twenty-four years."

"I find that hard to believe," he said. "You look much younger than twenty-four."

"What *I* find it hard to believe is that I'm stuck on an island with a meat-eating moron. A beef-eating buffoon."

"I'm really a good guy," he said.

As the sun began to sink behind the horizon, the sky turned rose pink with thin strips of purple. "Some people would envy us being on a deserted island away from the cold, cruel world," Evan remarked.

"I guess some stupid people would," Fanny said. "But even *this* isn't far away enough. My greedy bastard of a father tells me I'll be more forgiving as I get older, so I decided not to get older. I don't want to be forgiving of the top one percent who take away what rightfully belongs to people who struggle every day of their stinking lives. In case you haven't noticed, the lower class is expanding at an enormous rate."

"When you say *expanding*, you don't mean getting fat, right?" he asked.

"Right, douchebag."

"Well, obesity is *another* problem."

"I'll bet you weren't valedictorian and never volunteered at a food bank," Fanny conjectured.

"I'll bet you never rotated your tires," Evan responded.

"I'll bet you never donated blood," she stated. "I once donated so much blood that I passed out and was rushed to the stinking hospital. One of the damn nurses actually recognized me from the time I overdosed on Valium and vitriol and damn near exploded."

"Damn," Evan muttered.

"When did you become so vapid?" Fanny asked.

"Are you kidding? I'm the *opposite* of vapid, whatever that word happens to be. In time, you'll agree with me."

As they continued hurling insults at one another, the sky became a vast black backdrop for the stars that glittered like sequins. The moon was full, round, and radiant. "I love bathing in the light of the moon," Evan shared.

"Now you're a master poet," Fanny remarked.

"Isn't it amazing that the moon's gravity actually pulls the ocean? The water literally bulges toward the moon and follows it as the earth rotates."

"Fascinating," Fanny chirped with sarcasm.

"Lunar influences play such a vital part in the planet's ability to support life," he explained with enthusiasm. "I often wonder how it all works so smoothly, the entire solar system, the miracle of it."

"Here's what *I* wonder: I wonder if there's a preponderance of twins born in Twin Falls, Idaho." Fanny felt a deep sleep approaching as she tried to stifle a yawn. She didn't want to drift off to slumber because she was actually beginning to enjoy Evan's offbeat company. But in the end, lethargy won.

The following morning, Fanny awakened with the rising sun and felt profoundly relaxed, as if having slept for a month instead of a mere seven hours. The world seemed to be moving in exceedingly slow motion. The ocean was devoid of waves; even the trees seemed tranquilized.

Fanny realized she had dreamed about Evan. The dream was fuzzy; all she could recall was that she was attending a small gathering in black and white when a smiling Evan made an appearance and whisked her away to some other, extremely vibrant, colorful place.

She gazed at her fellow castaway, still asleep, obviously dreaming because his expression changed every few seconds. She couldn't help noticing his thick, tender lips, wondering why she hadn't noticed them before. Ever so gently, she placed her hand over his face, just inches away so that she could feel his breathing on her fingertips. When he began to stir, she swiftly backed away.

"Good morning," he mumbled as he opened an eye. "Are we still stranded?"

"Stranded and starving," she announced with faux cheer.

Evan lifted the top half of his body and looked out to the sea. Then he glanced at his partner in survival. Then, in a slow double-take, he looked back at the sea. "Is it my imagination or is there a boat out there?"

"I think there is," Fanny said. "But it's too far away. We wouldn't be able to get its attention."

Evan nodded in agreement. "How about breakfast?" he asked. "Should we go to the farmers market?"

"You are truly twisted."

"And you're brutally honest. I never met anybody like you."

"Is there a compliment buried somewhere in those words?"

"I need to urinate," he responded. Evan jumped up and jogged robustly to the sea. Fanny watched him, strangely mesmerized by his simplicity and his odd, childlike charm. She also began to appreciate his physicality, the way he slung his nimble, pliable body around.

When he was finished, he splashed cold water on his face. "Fanny!" he shouted with excitement. Slowly, she sauntered over. "It's definitely coming our way!"

With its large sail, the boat was undoubtedly heading toward the island. Evan started screaming and flailing his arms like a little boy trying to attract the attention of some movie superhero. "Over here! Over here!"

"I think they see us," Fanny nonchalantly said.

"This way!" Evan shouted.

As the boat approached, the large sail came clearly into focus. "My God," Evan whispered.

"My God," Fanny repeated.

Even looked incredulously from Fanny to the boat and back to Fanny again. "I don't believe my eyes," he gushed. "Is it what I think it is?"

"It can't be."

"No. It can't."

"But I think it is," Fanny said, stupefied.

"No," he responded.

"Yep."

"It's a mirage," Evan said. "A hallucination."

"Nope. It's a floating Starbucks."

"A floating Starbucks," he repeated.

"A fucking floating Starbucks."

The recognizable logo appeared boldly on the large sail. A young barista was busy at the cappuccino machine while a grinning guy in an apron steered the vessel.

As the boat was docking, the barista shouted to the castaways. "Can I start a beverage for you?"

"Tall non-fat latte!" Evan shouted back.

"Mocha cappuccino!" Fanny yelled. "Venti!"

With his heart racing, Evan spontaneously drew Fanny to him in an almost desperate embrace. Then the couple took a few steps toward the world's first waterborne coffee house.

Life and Breath

The Hollywood Freeway heading north was clogged with cars, vans, SUVs, and trucks. The vehicles were crawling, inch by endless inch, a sea of pebbles at the mercy of a sluggish Friday rush-hour tide. Vonda Elizabeth Barrett was boxed in by a moving van on her left and a Mack truck on her right, each the length of the Great Wall of China, or so it seemed. She tried to extricate herself from these mountains of steel, but it was impossible; she was resigned to the fact that if she dozed off and an accident occurred, she'd be crushed to a gory death, and that would be that. A grape squashed by the foot of a gorilla. No one would know she'd even *been* there.

Behind her smoky-goth eyes, royal-blue wig, and ruby-red lips, Vonda (birth name Verna) was a small-town girl who could hardly wait to create an alluring new identity and meet other misfits with similar offbeat cravings. Almost never out of costume, Halloween was a state of mind, her chosen way of life.

She realized this was a rebellion, a slap in the face to the bland life her parents had provided for her. Spending her adult years in Perkins, Nebraska, or some neighboring town would have been death by asphyxiation. Early on, this square peg trying to fit into society's round hole had made a choice. She chose life and breath.

When the traffic began to flow again, allowing vehicles to increase their speed significantly, Vonda pictured the edgy Standard Hotel with its white façade illuminated by spooky blue lights, and its quirky, eye-catching upside-down banner that, to the unsophisticated eye, seemed like a mistake. Perfectly suited to those longing for the fast-lane life, this was Vonda's destination. She would exit on Sunset Boulevard and then head west. With its live performance art, electric-blue Astroturf sundeck, and nightly DJ in the lobby, the Standard was no mere hotel; it was an endless party. Every single Friday night, the half-mile stretch of the Sunset Strip leading to the Standard was crowded with weekend cruisers. It was jammed with young partiers and industry peeps dripping in fur, ego, and bling, desperate to become part of the cutting edge. The men didn't wear overalls. The women didn't don housedresses. The neighbors didn't stare with disdain as if you were some weird, oddly dressed foreigner when all you did was throw on a lilac wig or apply a little too much rouge. Vonda found her proper place, inhabited by people who celebrated her creativity and quirkiness, people who saw their deepest selves in her many faces.

Vonda closed her eyes and imagined breathing in the hotel's heavily perfumed air that seemed imported from some magical, mystical place. The air never failed to envelope her with sublime comfort. With her first breath, she always felt a gigantic rush; she knew she was close to paradise. She inhaled a gust of twilight air, but it was merely exhaust fumes emerging from the vehicles of fellow travelers heading to downtown or San Pedro or north to the San Fernando Valley.

The very second Vonda opened her unsuspecting eyes, terror struck. Rapidly approaching a freeway overpass, shooting down at her like a missile from the sky, was a metal shopping cart that some sadistic psychopath had hurled over the edge. She tried swerving to the left, but she collided with a Humvee, and then the shopping cart struck the windshield of Vonda's car with fierce, deadly impact. A tour bus rammed into her from behind, and the sound she heard was booming, deafening. The noise was so startling that she didn't realize her body was in flight. Suspended. In radiant, bloody motion. Then came the screeching of metal from dozens of cars behind her and the blasting of horns like the brass section of an amateur orchestra attempting to play the same note. Like a flash frame in a movie, she caught a fleeting glimpse of her smiling parents on their front lawn before the screen abruptly cut to black.

In the end she was wrong. Many people knew Vonda Elizabeth Barrett had been there.

A Splash of Color

"I forgot what I remembered to tell you," Lauretta said to Ben as she began to unpack groceries from the brown paper bag on the kitchen counter. The classical radio station was playing a light, airy piece by Vivaldi, creating the impression of a lush green meadow with a nearby lake on which overdressed people were boating.

"What?" her husband asked without looking up from the sports section of the newspaper.

"As I was leaving the grocery store, I remembered something that I'd forgotten to tell you, and I meant to tell you as soon as I got home. But now that I'm home, I forgot what it was."

"It'll come back," Ben assured her, engrossed in an article about a baseball game in which his home team was slaughtered. Either his eyes or his gold-framed glasses were beginning to fail him. Even squinting, the words on the page were blurrier than they'd ever been before.

"Not after it went away," Lauretta said. "It rarely comes back after it goes away."

"For me, when it goes away it always comes back, usually at the most unexpected time," he said, lifting his legs to stretch out on the ultra-modern sofa with its tubular frame and clean, square lines, the one Lauretta insisted on buying despite the fact that it wasn't the most comfortable model in the showroom.

Lauretta's handsome, high-cheekboned face registered frustration as she yanked open the refrigerator door. Under the harsh kitchen light, she removed two fist-size heirloom tomatoes from the paper bag and placed them in the empty fruit compartment. In her off-white sweater dress, the honey-blonde homemaker blended in with her utilitarian kitchen, practically disappearing into its washed-out palette.

"What was the subject matter?" Ben asked, still in a depressed fog due to the dramatic defeat of his team.

"I don't remember, but it wouldn't matter if I did." She removed two fist-size Fuji apples and nestled them on top of the tomatoes.

"Of course it would matter," Ben calmly said. "It would help you remember what you forgot."

"No," she responded. "Let's say the subject matter was money, or Daniel. That wouldn't help me remember a bit."

"*Was* it Daniel?" Ben asked, finally looking up at his wife, realizing he hadn't spoken to his son in several days.

"I told you I don't remember."

"No," he corrected her. "You told me you *forgot* what you remembered. So, you did remember at a certain point."

"Well, not at *this* point," Lauretta said, a smidgen of anger seeping into her honeyed voice. "At this point, I have no recollection." She grabbed a package of lean ground beef from the bag with such force that her fingerprints became etched in it.

"But I don't think it had anything to do with Daniel, or Dartmouth."

Ben breathed a sigh of relief. He was now comfortably

ensconced on the somewhat uncomfortable sofa. "Did you see something at the store that bothered you? Was there an unpleasant encounter at the counter?"

"Actually there *was*," she stated. "But that has nothing to do with what I don't remember."

"What kind of encounter?"

"I was in the *Under Ten Items* line and the freckled girl at the check-out counter counted thirteen, but she was counting each orange as a separate item. Isn't that ridiculous?"

"Were all the oranges the same?" he asked. "Or was one Valencia and another navel?"

"Both were blood," she said, recalling that she avoided reaching for a bunch of purple grapes next to the almost-neon yellow bananas because they seemed to be moving. "I hate to shop on Saturday. Rude teenagers work the register. And today's teenagers are positively vile. You don't suppose Daniel is like that, do you?"

"Of course not. We raised him to be polite."

"But we have no idea what he's like behind our backs. He may put on a very convincing front until he's behind our backs."

Suddenly the refrigerator started humming like it was alive and breathing, giving Lauretta a slight jolt. She wondered whether other appliances might begin making weird noises. Then she realized she was being absurd, so she did her best to banish the thought.

A two-pound calf's liver wrapped in sturdy white butcher paper was her next item to unpack. She proceeded to store it in the cabinet above the sink. A few strands of hair fell over her eyes and she pushed them away with annoyance, accidentally hitting her forehead with the bottom of her wedding ring. The gray was invading her scalp gradually, like crabgrass on the front lawn, and she wondered whether Ben noticed. "You don't think of me as forty, do you?" she asked, struck by the realization that the journey from *I do* to *You don't think of me as forty* seemed to fly by in twenty weeks instead of twenty years.

"No, Lauretta," he replied in a reassuring tone. "I think of you as forty-one."

"Don't you think I look years younger?" She knew she did; she heard it from people all the time. But she wanted to hear it from Ben. She wanted him to notice that her dress size hadn't changed in two decades. "On a good day," she told him, "I can pass for twenty-nine."

"Whatever makes you happy," he mumbled.

That wasn't exactly the response she'd hoped for, so she chose not to tell Ben about the previous day's unintentional shoplifting incident for fear he'd think her mind was deteriorating. She honestly didn't remember putting the salmon-pink scarf in her jacket pocket. She recalled seeing it, touching it, even thinking it would be a perfect splash of color with her charcoal-gray blouse. But she could've sworn she placed it back on the shelf after glancing at the surprising three-hundred-dollar price tag.

She reached for another item in the brown paper bag, a sirloin steak big enough for two. "Will you go shopping with me next time?" she asked, fearful that she might see other fruit mysteriously moving in the produce department.

"Of course," he said. "But only if you go to the ball game with me next week." He knew she loathed sports, all sports, just like he loathed supermarkets.

"What kind of ball game?" she asked. "Foot? Base? Basket?" She honestly had no idea. Tossing or dribbling balls couldn't have been more sleep-inducing.

"You don't have to be a sports nut to know it's baseball season, Lauretta," he said in a condescending tone. "Everybody knows it's baseball season."

"Everybody except me," she said. "Does my refusal to sit through an interminable ball game mean you won't go shopping with me?"

"I'll go shopping with you, all right? But we'll go to the *regular* market instead of that health food store. I need a change from those sprouts and greens."

"Greens," Lauretta quietly said. "I think it had something to do with greens. *Celery* actually. She was chopping celery."

"Who?" Ben asked. "Who was chopping celery?"

"Valerie du Plexis Rose."

Ben froze. The pleasant classical piece playing on the radio came to an abrupt end, allowing the mournful moan of Rachmaninoff's Piano Concerto Number 3 to float through the air. "When did you see Valerie du Plexis Rose chopping celery?" he asked, alarmed.

It was coming back to her, slowly, clearly, each detail revealing itself in succession. "This morning I stopped off at her house. On Swansdown Drive."

"I know where her house is," he said, his spine stiffening.

"I realize that, Ben. I've realized that for several months." She noticed the refrigerator door was still open, so she slammed it with such force that the Scrabble set on top of the freezer fell to the terrazzo ceramic-tiled floor, dispersing dozens of small wooden letters. What she didn't notice was her husband's expression of horror.

"*What* exactly have you realized?" Ben asked with dread.

"You know that unique smell of water on cement?" Lauretta asked, ignoring the question. "Her sprinkler was going at full blast, hitting more sidewalk than grass. What a waste, especially in this drought." She paused for dramatic effect and got it; Ben could feel his blood pressure rising "The front door was unlocked, so I wandered in and followed what sounded like chopping. Sure enough, Valerie du Plexis Rose was chopping celery on the butcher-block island in her newly remodeled kitchen."

"Why did you go in the house?" Ben sternly asked.

She didn't tell him the truth. She didn't tell him that she was sick and tired of living a life of quiet desperation, and the time had come for *noise,* as loud and deafening as possible. "I don't know what you saw in that tramp," Lauretta said nonchalantly, "with those unnatural highlights and those phony lips. She had a plastic sheen, like processed cheese."

"*Had?* Why are you talking about her in the past tense?"

"She liked baseball," Lauretta stated. "That took me by surprise."

"How do you know she liked baseball?" Ben asked. He himself didn't know the answer.

It was only days earlier when Lauretta had overheard a conversation Valerie had with a feisty female pharmacist who was wearing a baseball cap emblazoned with the name of a local team. (Lauretta had been standing nearby with her back turned, pretending to compare pain relievers.) The pharmacist had commented on the team's triumphant performance the previous season, and Valerie had exclaimed, "Weren't they the best? I never miss a game."

But Lauretta chose not to share this story with Ben. Instead she focused on their exceedingly long marriage. "You dominated my life for over two decades," she reminded him, "decades of ups and downs and sickness and health and guilt and joy and godawful in-laws. I chose *wife and mother* as my primary roles. I *devoted* myself to..." She suddenly stopped talking. "Oh, what's the point?"

Lauretta vividly recalled her lunch with Santiago DeGeorge after going back to work at the real estate office the year Daniel entered high school. Santiago wasn't the least bit subtle about his desire to have an affair with her, but she flatly refused despite his swarthy good looks and gargantuan hands. Lauretta had honored the sanctity of her marriage. "We raised a son, and now that he's in college I thought we'd have time for each other," she explained. "You and me. Lauretta and Ben. Instead, you found time for Valerie du Plexis du fucking Rose with those phony breasts on display like an avant-garde sculpture."

"Lauretta, listen to me, please."

"She was surprised to see me," Lauretta interrupted, her pace quickening, "so she put the knife down and asked what I wanted."

"What *did* you want?" Ben inquired, now on the edge of the sofa.

"A cup of coffee. A pot was brewing, and you know how I love the smell of coffee. I desperately wanted a cup, so I asked her for one. 'All right,' she said in that husky, smoky voice of hers. When she turned toward the stove, I grabbed the knife she'd been using to chop celery. It was a lot heavier than it looked. Then she turned back in my direction and moved very fast, to fetch a cup I think, and as she approached me she accidentally impaled herself on the knife. It went all the way inside her, maybe even *through* her, through that teeny tiny waist."

"No," Ben said, panicked.

"Oh yes," Lauretta assured him. "Then I turned the knife clockwise. I'm not sure why I did that, but halfway around, I pulled it out. She looked at me with an odd expression: confused, quizzical, but also kind of impressed, like she admired me for having the guts to do such a thing."

"Admired you?"

"I honestly think she did," Lauretta stated with a satisfied grin. "You won't believe what happened next."

"I don't believe what happened *last*!" Ben exclaimed.

"Next, she gathered the little bit of strength she had left in her weak, withering body, and she punched me in the stomach, right smack in the gut like a professional boxer." Lauretta shut her eyes and shook her head from side to side. "Let me tell you—that hussy had a powerful left hook."

"No, no, no," Ben muttered.

"Oh yes, yes, yes," Lauretta insisted. She opened her eyes and took a step toward her horror-struck husband. "A person can only take so much, Ben. It was either me or her. Somebody had to win and somebody had to lose. You understand that, don't you?"

"No, I don't understand it," he said, in glazed terror.

"That's the way the world works!" she proclaimed. "You're a big boy, you should *know* that. I declared myself the winner, the victor, the conqueror."

"What did you do then?"

"Then I poured myself a cup of coffee. A fresh, delicious hot cup. Thankfully, she had soy milk in the refrigerator. I drank about half of it, then I got into the car and drove home fast but not *too* fast. The last thing I wanted was to get pulled over for a gosh-darn speeding ticket. So I turned on the radio and listened to some delightfully soothing classical music. Brahms, I think it was. Or maybe Debussy. Traffic was light, the air conditioning was heavenly, and the bloody knife was resting peacefully in the passenger seat." Suddenly Lauretta's eyes lit up like miniature lanterns. "The knife!" she shrieked. "In the passenger seat! There's blood all over the car, Ben! That's what I forgot to tell you!"

"Oh God," Ben said, standing up. "Oh my God."

"What time does the car wash on Witch Hazel close?" she asked.

Ben gazed at his wife with a combination of revulsion and rage. He reached for his mobile phone as he bolted out the front door.

Lauretta stood perfectly still, enjoying the surge of adrenaline her body was producing. She wasn't necessarily proud of the startling, bloody scene she'd caused, but she couldn't deny feeling a sense of supreme, sublime satisfaction.

Lauretta didn't realize she had one more item to unpack, a fist-size human fist, female, with several gold rings on its fingers, until its blood began seeping through the paper bag and dripping onto the white linoleum like thick crimson raindrops splashing onto a windshield. Then she placed it in the refrigerator next to the two sirloin steaks she'd purchased for a protein rich dinner.

Beautiful Ghost

The very second Susannah laid eyes on the young man meticulously packing her groceries into a sturdy, brown paper bag, she looked away. Could it be? Could *he* be? It was eleven years later. A different town. A different setting. He was too old to be Timothy's son, she surmised. A brother maybe? Cousin? Nailed to the white tile floor, she forced herself to look again. This time she noticed slight differences: the fuller lips, lankier frame. But he resembled Timothy in a truly startling way. Susannah's heart pounded with almost primal fury. She was suddenly sorry she'd purchased a box of Tampons.

The supermarket employee was a doppelganger for Timothy Ladd, the Goslar High School senior Susannah obsessively loved when she was seventeen, the one who took her on three dates, stole her very soul, and then hit the road with the older, more voluptuous Johanna Lussky. Nothing had ever hurt like Timothy's brusque rejection, his "I just don't see us going any further." Nothing had prepared a seventeen-year-old for such profound, debilitating anguish. "I felt *pain* when he left. Actual physical pain," she told her best friend Esperanza. "Nobody teaches this to you in school, how to cope with something like this."

"Do you need help to your car?" the young man politely asked as he placed the last item, a bar of hibiscus soap, into the bag. Too shaken to speak, Susannah nodded.

As soon as they stepped into the late afternoon sun, she spoke up. "By any chance, is your last name Ladd?"

"Nope," he told her. "Massey. Dylan Lloyd Massey."

A wave of relief washed over her. "Well, you look like someone I once knew."

"Oh cool," he said, suddenly sounding sixteen.

The leisurely stroll to the car gave *him* a chance to gaze at Susannah's ethereal exquisiteness. With her cascading orange-gold hair, delicate pink lips, and deep-set eyes that seemed sad despite the fact that they sparkled such brilliant blue, she had a dreamy, hurt quality. This pre-Raphaelite beauty had always been the most dazzling girl in the room - living room, bedroom, waiting room, powder room—and entering her thirties only enhanced her haunting allure.

A warm breeze blew as Susannah led Dylan to a spotless black Mercedes. The young man carefully placed the heavy bag in the back seat of the car as Susannah attempted to fix her windblown hair with two fingers. "Anything else I can do for you?" Dylan asked, imbuing as much innocence into his tone as he could to cover the question's not-so-subtle suggestiveness.

"Not right now, but thanks very much," Susannah said. She could feel his eager eyes undressing her as shoppers reached for boxes of laundry detergent just yards away. Susannah felt vibrantly awake, like her blood was flowing at an accelerated speed. Life had been devoid of this spectacular feeling for more than a decade; it was forgotten territory. Now it was back: the passionate, heart-pounding, thrilling, almost insatiable hunger.

"I only work here part time," Dylan announced as if apologizing for his plebeian status. "I plan to study medicine."

"Medicine," Susannah said with surprise, trying in vain to imagine this kid performing a transplant. "That takes dedication."

"When I commit to something, I give it my all," he announced, staring into her eyes with such blazing intensity that it almost came off as comical.

"I think you'll make an excellent doctor," she told him, quickly realizing she had absolutely no justification for this statement. Embarrassed and self-conscious, she turned away, climbed into the car and fastened her seatbelt.

"I think you're really beautiful," Dylan said, both hands leaning on the side of the Mercedes.

"Be good," she replied. Then she started the engine, maneuvered her wheels and stepped on the gas, appreciating the fact that her gushing admirer didn't say another word, that he didn't shout *I get off at six* or *Can we have coffee sometime?*

The boy didn't budge; he remained in a ruminative stance, watching his dream woman drive off as though making sure she'd exit the parking lot safely.

Gliding through her picturesque new neighborhood dotted with crooked trees and old-fashioned phone booths, the entire supermarket interaction seemed like a hazy, distant dream. But she clung to it like a life raft.

Susannah pulled into the driveway of the Spanish colonial house she shared with her attorney-husband, Neal. She opened the car door and seemed to float out as if weightless. The imprint of Dylan's right hand remained on the side of the car, a large hand, a large print, and Susannah gazed at it longingly. As soon as she realized the absurdity of this, she grabbed her groceries and headed into the house, walking past the defiant white-scalloped wall that seemed to imprison her on the property.

Over the next two days, she spent hours obsessing about the items she needed at the supermarket. The refrigerator was fully stocked, but she could always use more bottled water and sourdough bread. Still, she realized driving to the store with such a lame excuse was legitimate cause for more psychiatric counseling.

She knew, as any professional would tell her, this was a textbook case: Timothy was the one that got away, and here he was again in the body of Dylan Massey.

Ridiculously simple. But she was seventeen then; now she was thirty-one. Now she was married. Now she had a solid goal to build a reputation in a brand-new town.

Still, she danced by herself in the den to the music playing in her head. She dreamed about him—incoherent, oblique dreams she couldn't recall the next morning in any detail except that Dylan had been close to her. She took the bar of hibiscus soap she'd bought and placed it on her bedroom bookshelf simply because he had touched it. Neal didn't notice anything different about his wife except for the occasional faraway look in her eye, but he was accustomed to that. "You live in your own jagged universe," he often told her. This time, she tiptoed on its dangerous edge. This time, there was a certain excitement to the upheaval. She'd grown tired of the sameness of her daily existence, the monosyllabic dinner conversation, the self-involved spouse. She was convinced that the further she drew away from the mundane, the closer she got to true happiness.

She patiently waited three days in which the ticking of the large living room clock seemed mercilessly loud, three days in which every waking moment included the image of Dylan's face and the calming sound of his voice. Three days, and she legitimately needed jam and honey and oatmeal and eggs.

Adrenaline pumping, she made her way to the market. The drive seemed to fly by in seconds instead of ten minutes, and she was only dimly aware of traffic lights and pedestrians along the way. She took her time finding the perfect parking spot—a private one at the west end of the lot, under the shade of a towering sycamore tree.

As Susannah approached the entrance, she was hit with the unthinkable possibility that Dylan might not be there, that it could be his day off. The notion almost paralyzed her; she felt twice her weight and so weak that walking into the store felt like an attempt to lumber from one end of a swimming pool to the other.

The saliva drained from her mouth as Susannah grabbed a dark-green-plastic basket. Then, lips parched and heart racing, she glanced at the check-out area and didn't see him. After taking a deep, nervous breath, she hobbled to the produce department, where she absentmindedly chose a head of iceberg lettuce, some organic broccoli, and a bag of baby carrots. Then she glanced at the check-out area again. Still no sign of Dylan.

Panic rising, she wandered aimlessly past the pasta and the toothpaste, somehow finding her way to a display of silverware. She grabbed a steak knife and pricked her finger with it, hoping to draw blood. Why, she didn't know. The prick hurt, but blood didn't emerge. She raced away, as if escaping the Donner Party.

Moments later she found herself in front of the mayonnaise display, where she recalled how delicious mayonnaise made almost *anything.* She considered purchasing every single jar in the store. When she realized the utter foolishness of this, she left the aisle and her eyes instantly fell upon Dylan, busy bagging groceries. He had materialized, magically, so it seemed. Not only could Susannah breathe again, she was struck with such a fierce blast of joy she thought she might cry. She realized that she was powerless. Or *was* she? She'd been told by doctor after doctor that she could exert control. That's what had been drummed into her troubled head. And she'd believed it. Until now. How could she control *this?*

Nine items nested in her basket when it came time to check out. She could've marched to the express line, but that wasn't where Dylan was working. She stepped behind a short, white-haired woman with an almost-full shopping cart that included two dozen cans of cat food, three gallons of milk, and a mop.

When her eyes met Dylan's, the recognition was instant, as if he'd been dreaming about *her* the way she dreamed about *him*. He barely took his burning eyes off her while bagging the older woman's cat food. Then he smiled warmly when it came Susannah's turn to step up to the plate. "Do you need assistance to your car?" he asked with a smirk as subtle as a Lifetime movie.

"Yes, thank you," she said.

Dylan carried the two paper bags and gently placed them in the back seat of Susannah's car. Then he stood firmly opposite her, close enough to smell the floral fragrance she had dabbed on her neck. This mingling of entities, this spontaneous combustion, created palpable heat. "You probably think I'm too young for you," he said, certain that he wasn't. "I'm over eighteen," he stated with boyish bravado. "Isn't that what counts?"

"When you get older, you'll be able to answer that question truthfully," she told him as her eyes feasted on the smooth, taut skin and thick, wildish hair of a typical teenage boy. But it was *Timothy* standing in front of her, not Dylan. It was *Timothy* she would kiss if she kissed him, *Timothy* she would invite into the passenger seat of the car her husband had chosen for her.

"I'm not a virgin," he quietly proclaimed, his hazel eyes holding an almost heartbreaking expression of longing.

"You'll make some girl very happy," Susannah said. "Treat her nicely." She extended her right hand and Dylan held it like a precious gem. Then he noticed the jagged purple line on the inside of her wrist. "What's that?" he innocently asked.

"Just a silly old cut," she said as she pressed her left arm against her body, covering a similar bruise on that wrist.

He tenderly kissed the violet slash, and Susannah instinctively knew what lay ahead. If she gave herself to this boy in *any* way, if she allowed this unquenchable desire to take hold, if she so much as leaned into the warmth of his body, her life would have crumbled like a cupcake in a fist, right then and there in the west end of the supermarket parking lot in the fading late-afternoon sun. Nothing would have satisfied her short of lurching into the newly opened ravine with eyes shut, trusting Dylan/Timothy would scoop her in his youthful arms. She also understood that moving so blindly and daringly forward was a headlong rush toward destruction. This she knew as well as she'd known anything in a strange, turbulent life that contained more than its share of crushing sorrow and slow journeys back to sanity.

"We'd be very sorry," she said to him. "Nobody teaches this to you in school." She kissed him softly on the cheek. Then she closed her eyes and breathed him in as deeply as she could, into a place that would be his alone.

It seemed like an otherworldly force that compelled Susannah to turn from the beautiful young ghost and climb into her car without looking back.

From that point on, Susannah would shop at the market five miles down the road.

A Killer in the Park
on a Cloudy Afternoon

On a curiously warm but murky Friday afternoon in February, high-ranking executive Teresa Finzi-Contini decided to leave her corner office early and attempt to meet a stranger in the park. It had been an exceedingly stressful week in which she had to terminate one well-liked employee because of habitual lateness and one loathsome employee due to personal hygiene problems, and she desperately needed a diversion.

There were always strangers in this particular Beverly Hills park: good looking, average looking, tall, short, young, old, reading, texting, sipping coffee, meandering around, exposing themselves. Specific areas of the park were designated for specific activities. The cool, shady north side with its tall elm trees was where children played in sandboxes and swung on swings. The spacious east section was where clusters of canines sniffed and frolicked on the sparkling green grass. The south end was deemed the *dangerous* area where strangers with candy held court and sexual perverts flashed themselves to unsuspecting passersby. Teresa had always imagined these perverts to be decrepit old men until she heard about the nubile knockout named Galaxy, a voluptuous vixen who enjoyed unbuttoning her blouse to the delight of pubescent boys who occasionally left school early to sneak a peek at her sizable breasts.

Sitting on a green wooden bench in the east section, Teresa felt overdressed in a vintage beige linen blazer, pleated skirt, and pear-shaped gold earrings. The shoes were crimson-suede pumps. Her elegant attire made up for her pasty-white skin, dark circles under the eyes, and honey-brown hair that hung lifelessly like cooked capelli pasta. Except for the plum lipstick, which resembled the color of raw sirloin rather than that of the succulent fruit, she usually skipped makeup altogether, except on special occasions when she would inadvertently appear excessively rouged.

In her younger days, *radiant* was the word most often used to describe Teresa Finzi-Contini. She wasn't a classic beauty, but she was by far the most alluring girl at Pottstown High School in Pottstown, Pennsylvania. With sultry sea-green eyes and a statuesque figure, she definitely commanded attention. Her mother told her she possessed a special glow, her own personal spotlight. Then she woke up one morning middle-aged, puffy, and menopausal, stupefied to discover that her spotlight had dimmed to virtual darkness. She no longer identified with the body in which she was living. When it came to attractiveness, she felt she was running on fumes.

Teresa was living life on the sidelines, far from the madding crowd, no longer an active, vibrant participant in the world as she was in her younger days. At just nineteen, she dove into the deep end of adulthood during a freewheeling four-day weekend in Las Vegas. Teresa Finzi-Contini and Vincent Mancini fell in love at first touch when they brushed against each other in the crowded bar area of one of the happening clubs. The fact that he was eleven years her senior didn't make the slightest bit of difference; his sex appeal quotient was off the chart. Giving in to their tsunami-like lust, they spent the rest of the weekend barely more than six inches apart.

When Vince descended to his right knee and proposed marriage, it took Teresa a quarter of a millisecond to deliver the answer he hoped to hear. She could hardly wait to become Teresa Finzi-Contini Mancini. She didn't realize until several months later that her hormones had gotten mixed up with her brains.

The romance faded fast because of the cocaine, the crystal meth, and the opiates Vince popped like breath mints. Watching her husband lose himself in a once, twice, three times a day habit revolted Teresa, and her attempts to stop him proved futile. He repeatedly tried to convince her to join in; late one night he actually shoved her head onto the glass coffee table where the powder had been lined up with precision. The glass shattered, and a tiny piece lodged in her forehead, creating a permanent scar. (If she hadn't turned her head in the nick of time, her nose might have broken.)

With the writing large and legible on the wall, Teresa went back to school and devoted herself to her studies. Her diligence paid off. After earning two degrees, she worked her way up the corporate ladder in a Los Angeles marketing firm and never had to depend on a man, *any* man, for financial support again.

In her elegantly decorated corner office, Teresa was queen—making rules, breaking rules, barking orders. But behind her imperious manner, there was a genuinely caring person who found it difficult to fire people no matter how much they deserved to be axed. In addition to the two employees she'd recently terminated, there were two others she needed to let go, but she put that off until Monday because she preferred ruining *two* weekends instead of *four*.

Vince's drug addiction had traumatized Teresa to such a degree that she didn't look at another man for almost two years after the ink dried on the divorce papers. (Vince found a voluptuous new bride within six months.) When Teresa finally felt ready to date again, the men needed to be as different from Vince Mancini as possible: Greek, Japanese, Native American, drug free, short haired, or bald. She was expecting to find the same level of passion, the same intensity that she had with Vince, but she found herself perennially disappointed (though both Kenji Fujimoto and Cheyenne Manygoats made valiant attempts).

But that was years ago. Now the only time she felt a man's touch was when she was examined by her doctor. On weekends, her loneliness was so crushing that she often found herself short of breath and crying for no apparent reason. When she tried to imagine her future, all she saw were agonizing nights of solitude, one after the next, with nothing to look forward to. She seriously wondered whether her life was worth living without intimate human contact, without someone to care whether or not she had the flu, without being able to enjoy a slice of golden crusted, garlicky pizza because of her unrelenting stomach problems. She didn't understand how living life could make a person feel like the walking dead. Teresa glanced at the west side of the park and noticed a cluster of six Spanish nannies wheeling baby carriages. Dressed in black, each with a wavy dark mane and a ruby-red rose growing out of her hair, they resembled a gang of sweaty, knife-wielding nuns.

Whenever Teresa encountered a baby on the street or in a store, her heart seemed to drop several inches. In fact, all her organs suddenly felt loose, as though her body was falling apart from the inside. She was always certain she'd eventually meet a man to father a child, but that sweet dream had slipped away along with her prime. She couldn't comprehend how some women hired Guatemalan or El Salvadorian nannies (for whom English was a weak second language) and allowed them to raise their precious progeny while they worked absurdly long hours, sometimes not setting foot on their plush living room carpets until past nine at night. In Teresa's eyes, they were simply *part-time* mothers, women who parented on weekends and holidays. (The singular advantage to this situation was the growing number of bilingual children capable of ordering at any Argentinian restaurant.)

Teresa opened her leather bag and took out her compact to examine her face. She realized the plum lipstick was truly atrocious, so she smeared it off with her hand. Now her palm was stained, but she didn't care.

Not five minutes later, she detected a not-so-subtle scent of hot dogs. Sure enough, there was a vendor standing with his large metal cart a short distance away. He was loading a heap of sauerkraut on a hot dog for a young man in a football uniform. The young man was carrying a fiery-red helmet that he placed on the ground in order to eat his frankfurter while standing. He devoured it in sixty seconds flat.

Then he picked up his helmet and approached Teresa.

"Hey, you want me to get you a hot dog? You'll have to pay for it, but I can go get it for you. That Greek guy sells delicious ones."

"How do you know he's Greek?" she asked.

"His name is Antonopoulaidescukoolous or something like that."

"That's very kind of you," Teresa said, "but I don't eat hot dogs."

"Well, you're the one missing out," he told her. "Listen, I'm on my way to the linen store to buy a package of six king-size pillow cases. There's a sale on packages of six. You wanna join me?"

Teresa wondered if this guy was developmentally disabled. "Well," she hesitated, at a loss for words. "Sounds thrilling, but..."

"You see, I have two pillow cases at home," the young man continued. "They need to be replaced, and I was wondering what I could use an extra new pillow case for." He possessed a strangely sinister voice that belied his wholesome appearance: sandy-blond hair, steel-blue eyes, strong chin. "If I was withdrawing a lot of money from the bank, a pillow case would be a good place to store the loot, but I'm not withdrawing money from the bank today, ma'am," he said. "If I had hard candy to hand out to children, a pillow case would be a great place to store the sweets, but giving candy to kids isn't on my list of things to do today either. If I had a pile of human bones that needed to be transported to the city dump, a pillow case would make a perfect pouch, don't you think?"

"But that's not on your agenda either," Teresa said, playing along.

"Well, yes, that's actually on my agenda for today."

"Do you mean to tell me you're in possession of human bones?"

"I sure am, ma'am," he proudly replied.

"Did you murder someone?" she inquired, shifting awkwardly on the bench.

"No siree Bob. Not in the least," he adamantly stated. "I ended some bitch's life, but that doesn't mean I committed murder. I would never kill a bitch without her consent."

"You had the bitch's consent?" Teresa asked.

"Of course. She was a successful business executive who wanted to stop living, so I gave her a hand, that's all. I helped her, assisted, provided a service."

"Why do you refer to her as a bitch?"

"It's just a term of endearment for a dame, ma'am."

"I see," she said. "Would you do me a favor and stop calling me ma'am?"

"Sure thing," he said.

"Did you have sex with this... uh... business executive?"

"Yes, I did," he said, "but when she was still breathing. I'm no psycho."

"Of course not," Teresa said. "At least you didn't indulge in necrophilia."

"She wasn't black," he stated.

"Necrophilia has nothing to do with skin color. It's the act of having sex with a corpse," she explained.

"Oh. Well, I didn't do that either," he insisted.

"So you said."

"Wait a minute. Do you mean to tell me you wouldn't fuck a handsome man if he was lying dead in your bed? No, that doesn't sound right. Let's say you were a man.

Can you imagine yourself as a man for second?"

"I can try," she reluctantly agreed.

"Good. You wouldn't fuck the woman of your dreams if she was lying dead in your bed?"

"I wouldn't," Teresa stated. "For me, death is a deterrent when it comes to making love."

"I'm not saying she was dead for a couple of *weeks*. Let's say it was only a couple of *minutes*. Would you still not fuck her? Him?"

"I gave you my answer."

"Well, I didn't fuck her when she was dead," he adamantly stated. "She was still alive. Maybe just barely, but alive."

Revolted by this young man's words, Teresa took a moment to digest the insanity she was hearing. She considered calling the police, but she felt she needed more information. "What's your name?" she asked.

"Helmut," he said. "It's German."

"I assumed it wasn't Vietnamese."

"Helmut Heimbrecht."

"Well, Helmut, in order for her body to fit into a pillow case, you'd have to *dismember* her, wouldn't you?" she asked.

"That's what kept me busy all morning, lady. I dismembered the bitch with dignity."

"And how do you dismember a bitch with dignity?"

"You start with a dark room. Then you light a few scented candles, play the most patriotic music you can find—something they might play on the 4th of July—and take absolutely no enjoyment in the process."

"Was the dismembering difficult?"

"I had the proper power tools, so no, it wasn't," he

shared with satisfaction. "In fact, it went as smoothly as a dismembering could go. I did an excellent job, if I do say so myself." He didn't merely *enjoy* his crimes, he seemed to *relish* them. Teresa would have guessed that Helmut had never been good at anything in his young life, that he'd regularly been called a failure by teachers and parents. And now, he finally found something at which he excelled. "You know what the hardest part was?"

"No," she said. "What was the hardest part?"

"Getting this ugly purple smear off her hand. I had to use lots of turpentine."

Teresa quickly hid her right hand behind her back. Just then, a frisky black schnauzer trotted up to Helmut and began barking fiercely. The dog's owner, stout and friendly, immediately rushed over and grabbed the canine's leash. "I'm so sorry," he said. "She barks but doesn't bite."

"Just get that dirty mutt away from me," Helmut shouted.

"She happens to be a squeaky-clean standard schnauzer, not a dirty mutt," the guy explained as he led the pup away. "And she only barks at people with evil in them."

"Damn German dogs," Helmut mumbled, his face filled with contempt.

Teresa picked up the conversation where it was left off. "Do you actually think the bones of this deceased woman will fit into an ordinary pillow case?"

"Of course not," he said, still rankled by the unpleasant canine encounter. "That's why I plan to buy a package of *six*. I'll need *three* to accommodate her."

"I see."

"And don't forget they're king-size," Helmut reminded her. "To be honest, I would've preferred throwing her out the window. I *love* throwing things out windows, but she didn't want her guts to be splattered all over the street."

"I can understand that," Teresa said. "On an ordinary day, what do you like to throw out the window?"

"Books, shoes, candles, pickles, the occasional lamp."

"The act of throwing things out a window is called *defenestration*, in case you didn't know."

"I didn't know that," Helmut said, "but thanks. You're a smart dame, you know that? *Defenestration*. I guess that makes me a defenestrator."

"I guess it does."

"Anyway, I'll still have one extra pillow case when I'm done, and I won't know what the heck to do with it."

"I'm sure you'll come up with something," Teresa remarked. "You seem like a resourceful fellow."

"I'm the most resourceful fellow you'll ever meet," he boasted. "And I happen to be looking for a place to use my resources. You're a lady executive, right?"

"I guess you could call me that," she said with hesitation.

"You have any jobs available?"

"As a matter of fact, I terminated two people this week and need to let two more go on Monday. So, yes, I do. Unfortunately, I have no need for someone with, uh, your qualifications."

"If you think all I do is dismember people, play football, and defenestrate, you're dead wrong, lady," he said. "It just so happens that I studied calculus and origami. Plus, I excel at Microsoft Excel. Before I turned twenty, I made it halfway up Mount Everest and *all* the way up the Statue of Liberty."

"Impressive."

"Damn right. Soon I'll be out of landmarks to climb halfway."

"I'll give you my card," Teresa offered, at a loss for anything else to say. "You can call me next week unless you want to have sex before then."

"Let's have sex before then," he suggested with guarded excitement.

"Really?" she asked with surprise. "Are you sure you want to have sex with *me*?"

"I'm an all-American male," he stated with pride. "Can we go back to your place?"

"I can't think of one reason why not," she said, suddenly starving, famished, and ready.

A wave of raucous laughter emerged from the group of nannies, and for a quick second Teresa thought they were laughing at *her*. Then she realized she was being ridiculous.

"Do you have enough pillow cases?" Helmut asked.

"If I'm not mistaken, I have all the pillow cases you'll need."

"But what if I need an extra one?" he asked. "What should I do then?"

"It just so happens that I bought an extra set of jumbo pillow cases not that long ago," she announced. "They're in the linen closet, right behind the pergola pink bath towels."

"Perfect," he said.

"The linen closet is right between the master bedroom and the bathroom."

Again, loud laughter erupted from the nannies. Teresa

glanced over. "I wonder what's so funny."

"One of them probably told a filthy joke."

"You don't suppose they're laughing at *us*, do you?"

"Why would they be laughing at us? They probably *envy* us!"

"A barbaric, necrophiliac miscreant and a desperate, aging executive? I guess so."

"Told you," he said. "Ready for liftoff?"

"Almost," she said.

"What else do you need to do?" Helmut asked.

"I need to look at this park one final time, really breathe it in." She had come to love this park, its beauty, its quiet, its sense of community.

"Then go ahead," he said. "Breathe."

Teresa's senses feasted on the lush green grass (much of it fake, she assumed, to be so majestically green in February), the sweet floral scent permeating the air, the striking old elm trees that survived one brutal winter after another.

In the east section, a half-dozen dogs frolicked.

In the south section, a man in a crimson coat was reading a book. Two large, dark clouds had formed in the sky directly above him, bringing a harsh chill and the likelihood of rain.

"We better start moving before we get caught in a deluge," Teresa said.

"Deluge?" Helmut quizzically asked as if he didn't know what the word meant.

"A downpour of rain," she explained.

"Right. We don't want to get soaked in a deluge," he said. "Hey, if a deluge happens at night, is it a nightluge?"

"Day or night it's a deluge," she informed him. "We

should leave right now, this very second, before the precipitation hits along with the wind, cold, thunder, lightning, misery, hardship, agony, anguish, torment, heartache, and rage."

"Let's vamoose!" he shouted.

A rush of adrenaline pushed Teresa to run as fast as she possibly could. But running on grass in designer heels wasn't particularly easy, so she removed her shoes and forged ahead at twice the speed. Helmut raced to keep up.

One of the nannies noticed the tumult and alerted the others. They erroneously assumed the well-dressed older woman was trying to get away from the athletic young man. The nannies began running to the rescue but there was no contest. They were much too slow to catch up.

The mismatched couple jumped into Teresa's waiting vehicle and took off. At that moment, Teresa could not have cared less about traffic safety. She drove almost recklessly, speeding through red lights, ignoring stop signs, excited by the options that lay ahead.

"You're a speed demon," Helmut said with a sly grin.

"When I *want* to be," she told him.

"Cool. We both like living on the edge."

Teresa began the ascent up Laurel Canyon, the road twisting and turning as she climbed higher and higher. The mountain was dotted with houses, some plain, some majestic, some so frail and flimsy that they seemed susceptible to sliding down the hill in a torrential rain. She noticed that her gas tank was almost empty, but there was enough to make it home, and that was all that mattered.

Suddenly a helicopter was hovering overhead, and Teresa's paranoia was such that she assumed *she* was the one they were searching for, though she had no idea why. Her body tensed. Heart pounded. When the helicopter flew south and out of sight, she noticeably relaxed.

Teresa's car crackled along, gaining speed, gaining altitude, heading to the summit, heading to her destiny, as the dark clouds finally burst open and drenched the hillside with the heaviest downpour of rain the city had seen in a great many months.

Gypsy Woman

Raven-haired, large-breasted, and tan as a leather wallet, some people guessed Mariella Brazzi was of Italian descent. Others put their money on Spanish, Greek, Middle Eastern or some exotic combination. With rings on eight fingers, bracelets on each wrist, loopy gold earrings, and a phalanx of necklaces, this ripe, robust woman was a walking nightmare for airport security.

Ironically, the restaurant she owned didn't reflect her flamboyant appearance.

Fabric-covered walls of pale yellow, a sizeable stone fireplace, and glass tables with crisp, white linens contributed to the decidedly elegant ambience. Mariella knew that a gaudy, garish décor would alienate her discerning customers.

The stranger who called on the phone was supposed to meet Mariella at four. At five minutes past the hour, the front door of Pietro opened to reveal a mousy woman of thirty-two in clothing the color of weak tea. Her dirty-blonde hair was lifeless, her skin pale. "You must be Mariella," she nervously said.

"Mariella Brazzi, the one and only," she responded in her husky, heavily accented voice.

"I'm Sally Mumford. It's um... very nice to meet you."

"Yes, well let's sit down, Sally Mumford," Mariella said impatiently. She wasn't expecting a tongue-pierced biker chick in denim, but this frail, fumbling creature was quite a surprise. "Coffee? Tea? Maybe cup of pumpkin soup?"

"Tea would be... uh, yes, tea would be nice," Sally said like a timid schoolgirl.

"Robby baby!" Mariella shouted to a short young man in an apron. "Two cups cranberry tea!"

"Got it," Robby shouted back.

Unlike the strange bird perched across from her, Mariella possessed a boundless capacity for enjoying life. She didn't just throw a party; she *was* the party. When patrons stepped into Pietro for dinner, they came for more than the food. They craved the woman's company, even if it was only a five-minute visit here and a two-minute visit there. It was as if her lust for living rubbed off on them.

"I appreciate your willingness to meet me," Sally offered.

"When stranger calls and says she found something that belongs to you, curiosity is aroused, no?"

"Well, I was hoping," she responded, tilting her head. She seemed to glance around the room every few seconds, causing her to appear even more nervous than she actually was. "I love the way you're dressed. You look like an exotic gypsy."

"I like color, the brighter the better. You look like you're allergic to everything except beige."

"Oh, no not really," Sally said, smoothing a sleeve of her solid beige blouse.

"So how long you plan to keep me in suspense?" Mariella inquired. "Tell your story, sweetheart."

Sally inhaled deeply, then exhaled slowly. She was obviously having trouble beginning the tale. Mariella leaned in closer, trying to find some clue to this peculiar woman's thoughts. She found nothing. "It's a little crazy," Sally finally said.

"So am I," Mariella assured her. "So don't worry."

"All right." Sally took another deep breath. "Well, a few weeks ago, I needed to look up a name in the telephone book. So I opened it to B, and the first name I came across, the very first one, was Mariella Brazzi."

"No kidding!" Mariella barked.

"It's true. Mariella Brazzi. I said the name out loud over and over. I thought it was the most beautiful name I'd ever heard."

"Thank you," Mariella said. "I like it, too."

"Now fast forward to the following week."

"If you say so."

"I do," Sally said. "I was driving to Palm Springs. Have you ever driven to Palm Springs?"

"Yes, I like desert. Please continue."

"Well, in the middle of that endless, flat stretch of highway, I felt a panic attack approaching, so I pulled over, got out of the car, and went into a meditation." Suddenly she stopped speaking and glanced around the restaurant yet again. "I'm sorry, but may I use the rest room for a quick minute?"

Mariella pointed. "Down hallway on left."

Sally clumsily stood up and hurried away as Robby marched over with two cups of piping hot cranberry tea on purple saucers. "Everything all right?" he asked in a conspiratorial tone.

"She's a fruitcake, but harmless. Go home."

"You sure?"

"I'm sure. Your new baby wants to see her daddy."

With a satisfied grin, Robby left the premises. When Sally returned to the table, Mariella noticed that her guest had neglected to button one of the sleeves on her blouse. "Darling," Mariella said as she observed a pale pink, horizontal scar on Sally's left wrist. She also saw that the woman's fingers were bare. An unmarried woman. "Darling, please finish story for me."

"Yes. Let's see, where was I?" she asked in a low, muffled voice.

"In desert."

"Yes, I'm in the desert, meditating. After the meditation, transcendental by the way, I opened my eyes and noticed a vial of pills on a patch of dirt a few feet away. I crawled over and grabbed it."

"You crawled on dirt in desert?"

"I was already on the ground, and it seemed easier than standing up. I looked at the bottle and was stunned to see the name Mariella Brazzi on it. Well, I just about died. 'This is too weird,' I said. I actually said those words out loud."

"I'm sure you did."

All of a sudden Mariella sensed the brutal solitude of a woman who admitted talking to herself twice within a period of five minutes. She hoped Sally Mumford didn't dance with a phantom boyfriend or send herself flowers on Valentine's Day.

"I was sure the universe was bringing Mariella Brazzi to me," Sally continued, "practically delivering her to my doorstep." She reached into her leather tote bag and rummaged around, searching for the pill container. While doing this, she noticed the open button on her sleeve and quickly took care of it.

"Ah, the evidence," Mariella exclaimed as Sally handed her the bottle. "Yes, is mine. Nicholas and I drove to Palm Springs last year. I don't remember throwing out car window, but is possible."

"I've never been someone who believed in mystical or paranormal activity, so the fact that I found this after seeing your name in the phone book was pretty darn unusual."

"Pretty darn," Mariella said. "And you decided to pick up telephone."

"Obviously I knew your number was listed, but it took me a while to work up the courage."

"You pop a lot of pills?" Mariella asked.

"I beg your pardon?"

"Anybody who crawls to bottle of pills in desert is hoping there will be some inside, no?"

Flustered, Sally picked up a cube of sugar and held it between her fingers. "I don't take any more than the average person." Instead of dropping the cube in her cup, she placed it back into the bowl. "Do you understand the point of my little saga?"

"Of course I understand. I'm not stupid," Mariella said. "Some people believe in coincidence and some don't. Some think everything happens for a reason, and others think there's no reason for anything."

"Which category do you fall into?" Sally asked.

"Oh, I think everything happens for a reason."

With a sigh of relief, Sally said, "I'm glad to hear that or this visit would've been a waste of time."

"I give you example. A few months ago, I discovered Nicholas screwing young freckled florist down the street. The bitch is barely twenty. I threw him the hell out of my house. See? A reason."

Sally seemed bewildered. She suspected she was being made fun of, but she wasn't entirely sure. "You think it was all in my head?"

"Maybe you needed to learn that there's no explanation for *anything* in this world. A house burns to ground in terrible fire but house next door is fine. You think the family who lived in burned house were bad people?" Mariella asked. "A psycho guns down a dozen students on college campus, but some girl standing there isn't hit. You think she's better person than the dead ones?"

Sally was quiet for a few reflective moments. "Your points are well taken," she said. "Suddenly I feel rather foolish."

"No reason to feel foolish. It's all chance, like game of cards."

"But in a game of cards, you can use your wits to help you win."

"In game of cards," Mariella declared, "the card you pick from top of deck is luck of the draw."

Standing up, Sally flashed a nervous fraction of a smile. "Thank you for meeting me, Mariella Brazzi."

"Leaving so fast?"

Sally nodded. It was obvious there was absolutely no chemistry or buoyant camaraderie between the two. They would not go shopping together or gab on the phone every night. Still, Mariella hadn't meant to cause anxiety; all she intended to do was speak the truth. Obviously, her truth was too harsh for the wobbly young woman in colorless clothing.

"I will walk you out," Mariella said, rising from the

table and heading to the door with determination.

As soon as they hit the pavement, Sally politely offered her hand, and Mariella clutched it with unexpected force. "Some people believe wearing yellow is good for the gallbladder. You think the gallbladder gives a crap what color you have on?"

"I guess not," Sally politely said.

Mariella closed her eyes and took a giant breath, still holding her visitor's hand. "It was very beautiful, sunny day like today."

"Excuse me?" Sally asked. "*What* was a beautiful sunny day?"

Slowly she opened her eyes, now strangely wet, and wistfully looked into the distance. A plane was flying from east to west, the only movement in the gigantic, clear-blue sky. "One day eleven years ago," she said, gently letting go of Sally's hand. "Seems like yesterday. Not far from here. The love of my entire life, my nine-year-old Pietro, was playing with best friend Casey Davis on grass in front. Throws ball back and forth. I'm on patio chair, keeping an eye on them. Telephone rings, so I run into house. My annoying sister Antonietta. I tell her I call back later. Then I walk back outside. I'm gone thirty seconds. During that time, ball flew into street. Pietro chased it, and a speeding car hit him."

"Oh God, no," Sally mumbled.

"You tell me. Why was he standing closer to street than Casey Davis? Do you think that was meant to be, the way you found pill bottle in desert? Do you think powerful hand of fate put him in that spot so he would run into road? Do you think drunk driver with suspended license was on street at exact time so he could run down my boy?" She felt the heat of the sun on her bronzed arms, and it soothed her. "Tell me something," she said. "Do you think I blamed my sister for calling on telephone?"

"I don't know. *Did* you?"

"You bet your ass I did!" Mariella shouted. "I say to her 'Why the hell you call in middle of afternoon? Why you bother me?' She had nothing important to tell me. Every single day, year after year, I blame selfish, stupid sister. Then one day I realize all she did was call on telephone. Why didn't I let damn thing ring? My fault, baby. Nobody else's," she declared. "Things happen, and you have two choices. You can pull your hair out, or you can keep going. I pulled hair out for long time until I realized I don't look good bald."

"I'm so sorry for your loss," Sally softly said. "I can't imagine the pain."

"To drive all the way out here looking for answers, you have pain of your own. Just remember you can't make sense of the impossible."

Sally nodded with sincerity. "I won't try to anymore."

The horn of a passing car honked twice. Mariella glanced over and waved politely, the way a Miss America would greet a group of admirers. Very quietly, she said, "No idea who that is. But everybody knows me, so I pretend to know them." When the car had passed, she stretched her arms out as if ready to hug the world. "There is much to enjoy," she said. "You understand?"

"Sometimes," Sally said.

"More than sometimes."

"I'll try."

"Don't try," Mariella barked. "Do it."

"Yes, all right." Sally held Mariella's gaze. "May I come

by the restaurant once in a while?" she asked.

"Anytime you like. Next time you try steak au Mediera."

"I don't eat meat," Sally said. "Sorry."

"Then I make you delicious aubergine. Eggplant, with sprouts and beans."

"Eggplant would be perfect."

"And buy colorful dress," Mariella ordered. "Blue, green, shocking pink."

"Shocking pink?"

"Well, *pale* pink."

Mariella knew the fussy vegetarian would never wear anything but her demure plain-Jane outfits and she would never set foot in the restaurant again. She knew this would be the first and last time they would see one another. "I need to get ready for dinner shift, young lady. Very busy dinner shift."

Sally gently embraced Mariella, and the hug lasted longer than either would've predicted. When it was time to part, Mariella broke away and opened the door to Pietro. She hurried inside without looking back.

Gawk

"Don't be afraid if the kids at school stare at you," Craig Farrell warned his five-year-old son, Lucas. "You were born different, that's all. Not better, not worse. Just different."

"Why?" the boy asked, his huge Bambi eyes so curious, so vulnerable.

"There's no explanation," his mother, Barbara, replied. "It's just unusual to have an extra finger on your left hand, that's all."

"And since it's a few inches longer than your other fingers, some people might be scared of it," Craig added, "even though there's nothing to be scared of, right?"

"Right," Lucas said.

"In the future, an extra finger might come in handy," Barbara told her son. "If you want to point at something, you'll be able to point with emphasis."

"Do you know what *emphasis* means?" Craig asked.

"It's the first letter of Monica's name."

"Oh, M for sis," Craig said with a proud smile. "Very clever, but that's not what it means. Emphasis means giving extra stress or power to a word or action."

Lucas tried his best to keep his extra finger a secret, but the digit was impossible to hide every minute of every day. The kids at Short Elementary School sometimes mocked and ridiculed him. "The only job you'll get is in the circus," some smart aleck would say. Small groups of boys would deliberately bump into him, causing his books to fly and his hands to reach out and grab them. One of the girls would inadvertently shriek when she saw the mutant finger, causing a minor commotion.

The young boy taught himself to eat with his right hand. (At the dinner table, his left rested in a fist.) Though it was his natural inclination to grab a pen with his left hand, he forced himself to write with his right. In order to make him feel more comfortable, his sister, Monica, copied him; she ate with her right hand and chose to write with her right hand even though her natural inclination, like her brother's, was to go left. Their parents were committed right-handers, but the grandfathers on both sides of the family were radical leftists at a time when left-handed people were thought to have been cursed by the devil.

Lucas felt like a freak, a bizarre object of derision. He couldn't understand why he was chosen out of everyone on the planet to cope with such a weird, embarrassing deformity. Every night before going to sleep, he prayed to wake up with ten fingers instead of eleven. Some nights, he prayed not to wake up at all.

When Lucas was eight, his mother walked into the downstairs bathroom and came upon a shocking portrait in red. Her son was sitting on the floor, a kitchen knife in his right hand, blood covering his small body. After cleaning and bandaging him, she explained, "You can't just lop off your finger, honey. It's a part of you. The medical term is polydactylism. Other people cope with it, too."

"No way," he said with excitement. "Other people

have an extra finger?"

"People have all sorts of deformities," his mother assured him. "Someday you might be able to have reconstructive surgery, but so far we haven't found a doctor willing to perform that particular operation."

"We might find somebody someday?" he asked, hope in his eyes.

"Oh yes, absolutely. Someday."

Lucas became expert at hiding his extra finger. Wearing winter gloves began in the autumn of each year and didn't end until spring had officially arrived, no matter how warm the weather had become. If he had to hold hands with someone during a fire drill, he made sure it was his *right* that was offered. And if someone asked him to play patty cake, he simply refused.

Lucas's best friend, Joey, couldn't have cared less about the extra digit. "My cousin Howard has three nipples and my other cousin Sarah has two lungs."

"We're *supposed to* have two lungs," Lucas told him.

"Oh right. Then maybe she has only one. Or three."

When he turned fifteen, Lucas shot up an entire eight inches, his voice deepened, and he began to show the first signs of facial hair. No one took more notice than the wavy-haired Paloma Gilbert, the prettiest girl in Lucas's class. "Do you want to be my boyfriend?" she asked one sunny morning in the schoolyard.

"Sure," he replied.

"Do you know why I like you?"

"Not really," he admitted.

"Because all the kids think you're grotesque, but you still show up every single day. That shows confidence, and I like confident men." This was the first time anyone ever referred to Lucas as a man, and he felt a powerful surge of pride. For the rest of the day, he strolled the school hallways with his shoulders back and manly chin held high.

"Why are you walking so weird?" Joey asked.

"Stiff neck," Lucas replied.

An outstanding student, Lucas excelled in science, math, and art. (In first grade, he'd been a wizard at finger painting.) He thought education was the greatest thing ever invented, with the possible exception of sex. Lucas was pretty sure he understood the machinations of making love, but he was desperate to experience it. Unfortunately, kissing with her mouth closed was as far as Paloma Gilbert would let him go. "I cannot take the slightest chance of becoming pregnant," she explained. "That would tie me down for at least ten years, and I need that decade to make a name for myself in the fashion industry."

"I'm sure people in the fashion industry have sex," Lucas said.

"Lucas, I just can't risk getting knocked up."

At that moment, Lucas understood that nothing of an intimate nature would take place with Paloma until they were both pushing thirty.

Though it frightened most people, Lucas's eleventh finger fascinated Irma Jonagold, a blowsy, brassy neighbor, pushing forty, who paid Lucas generously to mow her lawn once a month.

One murky Saturday morning, Lucas finished cutting Irma's grass. Despite being sweaty and exhausted, he was invited in for breakfast. Expecting to enter a haven of edible delights—eggs scrambling, bacon sizzling, bread toasting—he was taken aback to see nothing on the stove and not a morsel of food on the kitchen table. The lady of the house, peering out of purple eye shadow, was dressed in a sheer pink blouse and short shorts that exposed her fleshy thighs. Though she tried to be frilly and feminine, she came across as coarse and gutsy, and she reeked of raw hamburger meat.

"Is Mr. Jonagold around?" Lucas asked. "Or the twins?" Mr. Jonagold was a jovial guy with a booming voice. The twins were curly-haired, rowdy seven-year-olds.

"Mr. Jonagold is meeting with an attorney in West Mineral, just outside Wichita," Irma explained. "Babette and Britney are spending the weekend with their twin cousins Oona and Parker in West Conshohocken. They have a Ping Pong table."

"Cool," Lucas said.

"Twins run in the family. And let me tell you—giving birth to them is pure hell. Can you imagine two human heads trying to emerge from a keyhole?"

"No, I really can't."

"Nobody can. Here's a bottle of water," she said, removing it from the refrigerator. "Come to the couch. Make yourself comfy."

Lucas followed Irma into the living room.

There were dirty plates on the coffee table, empty beer bottles next to half-eaten boxes of chocolates, and frilly dolls strewn all over the room, most of which belonged to Irma, not the twins. The place was a complete mess. Lucas could've made himself more comfortable on a bed of six-inch nails, but Irma made herself comfy enough for the two of them, snuggling up to her guest on the worn sectional sofa.

"Now give me your paw, puppy dog."

Lucas instinctively lifted his right hand.

"No, silly boy," Irma barked. "The one with the extra finger."

Hesitantly, Lucas lifted his left hand and Irma clutched it as she crossed her legs. "This extra pointer sets you apart from every stupid geek in this godforsaken town. Don't you forget that."

"Mayor Plunkett thinks I'm a freak," he confessed.

"Mayor Plunkett is a pathetic nitwit who only got elected because his competition was a money launderer," she responded.

"Harriet Moody throws herring at me when I walk past her fish market."

"Harriet Moody is going through menopause." Irma shared. "I think you're a boy wonder, that's what *I* think. That big finger allows you to manipulate certain things, *jostle* them, if you will."

"Really?" he asked with a tremulous smile.

"Really truly. Now *will* you?" she coyly inquired.

"Will I what?"

"Jostle for me?"

"What do you want me to jostle?" he asked.

Irma uncrossed her legs slowly and arched her back suggestively. "Let's not beat around my bush, you luscious piece of pumpkin pie," she cooed. "You'd like to thrust that digit of yours inside me. Am I right or am I right?"

"I guess you're right," Lucas said, feeling more than a bit on edge. He lifted his hand and gently stuck his aberrant finger into Irma's watery mouth. The moment it touched her tongue, he pulled out. "Listen," he said, voice quivering, "I have to go work on my science project. I'm trying to win the fair." He swiftly rose from the sofa and zoomed from the house like a terrified horse running from a burning stable. He would never mow the Jonagold lawn again.

*

Lucas's chaste and restrained romance with Paloma Gilbert was progressing nicely when a nasty rumor began to circulate. "She's doing it with Miles Tanza," Joey announced to his buddy. Miles was a football player with muscular shoulders and a cleft in his chin. Most of the girls became woozy when he merely looked in their direction.

"She would've told me," Lucas said.

"Doubtful, bro."

"But she made a vow to keep her clothes on at all times."

"Maybe she meant all times except when she's in Miles Tanza's bed."

"No, she would do anything to avoid getting pregnant," he said.

"Maybe to avoid getting pregnant by *you*, bro."

The shock of this truth was like a boulder being dropped on Lucas's head. *Why would Paloma want to risk having a mutant baby with eleven fingers? Why would any girl be willing to risk that?* he thought.

Lucas stopped calling Paloma, and she made no effort to contact *him*. The rumor turned out to be true. Paloma and Miles became a hot item. The kids at school even came up with a nickname for them: Piles.

*

Soon after turning eighteen, Lucas was thumbing through the *Portsmouth Post* when an article about an organization called Persons With Deformities caught his eye.

Interviewed was a young woman who was born with webbed hands and feet. "I was horrified by the way I looked for ten years," Olive Barnes said. "Then one day, I noticed a beautiful cloud in the sky that was shaped like my hand, and I began to think of my body as an enchanting, inventive sculpture." Lucas found this woman and her words inspiring.

The organization's annual conference was being held the following afternoon at a hotel in Concord. There was no doubt in Lucas's mind that he would attend. He checked the train schedule and decided to catch the 9:00 a.m. to New Hampshire's capital city.

When Lucas stepped into the lobby of the ornately decorated, old-fashioned hotel, he was struck by the gold carpet that seemed to stretch for miles. Off to one side was an elegant little restaurant serving food to a predominantly white-haired crowd. The other side consisted of a bank of elevators and a bank of desks: registration, concierge, information, valet. He wouldn't have been surprised to see an actual *bank*. Each desk, made of dark cherry wood, was intimidating either by its size or the stringent, no-nonsense employee behind it.

Lucas had no idea where to go, so he approached the information desk. "Excuse me," he said.

The man behind the sturdy desk took a few seconds

before looking up from the magazine he was engrossed in reading. "May I help you?" he asked, obviously annoyed.

"Yes. I'm looking for... well, it's a group of people having a conference."

"Could you perchance narrow it down for me?" he asked condescendingly.

"There's a meeting that's supposed to start at noon," he explained. "In this hotel."

"Schedule of events is posted right there." He pointed to a glass-enclosed sign hanging on the wall a few yards away.

"Thanks," Lucas said. He rushed over and saw that the meeting was being held in the Mesopotamian Room on the mezzanine level. Instead of waiting for the elevator, he ran up the gold-carpeted steps two at a time, heart pounding with anticipation, ready to enter what promised to be a brand-new, exciting world.

When he entered the spacious room, Lucas was nearly blinded by wide white smiles welcoming him warmly. He wandered around under the fluorescent lights, nodding at these exceedingly nice people, aged eighteen to eighty, every one of them living with some form of physical deformity. His eyes danced the way a child's would in an awesome new toy store; he didn't know where to look next.

Speeches began. Standing behind the podium, an eight-foot-tall man with gigantism talked candidly about his extreme height as well as his former drug addiction. "A lot of us had shaky starts," he said. "Then some of us went downhill fast."

A bowlegged woman with vitiligo admitted to being a former prostitute. "I had sex with conjoined twins, dwarfs, and transsexuals. I became a Diane Arbus photograph," she said with a chuckle.

A middle-aged man with a misshapen chest due to pectus excavatum confessed to being a recovering alcoholic. "I had to do *something* to take my mind off my deformity," he said, "and drinking was a lot easier than learning Mandarin." These were no angels, no martyrs, just real people coping with challenging situations, human beings who happened to be mangled by life. Every one of them refused to be called a victim. Every one of them managed to incorporate his or her anomaly into a rich, productive existence.

Following the final speaker, the attendees (except those with severe foot deformities) milled about the large room, sipping sodas and munching on snacks.

From a few feet away, Lucas recognized the young woman who was interviewed by the *Post*. "I read about you in the newspaper," he said excitedly, as if she were a celebrity.

Amazed, she giggled. "I'm so glad you read it."

"That's why I'm here. Your name is Olive Barnes." She was almost as tall as Lucas with big, soulful eyes and a mouth that appeared lavender.

"You even remembered my name," she said with wonder.

"Mine's Lucas Farrell," he said, offering his right hand, momentarily forgetting his new acquaintance had no fingers.

She gently shook his hand and smiled widely, showing off a set of perfect, snow-white teeth. The feel of her hand was foreign, unfamiliar, like that of the wing of a bird or the gill of a fish. Lucas didn't dare look down; he held

Olive's gaze, which was bubbling with interest.

"Tell me something about yourself," Lucas said. "Any old thing."

"Sorry to disappoint you, but unlike the people who spoke at the podium, I'm not a hooker or a heroin addict. I lead a terribly boring life. I go to school, watch TV, and still live with my parents at age twenty. Pathetic, huh?"

"Not pathetic at all," he replied. "I think it's just fine." Lucas and Olive moved their conversation to the hotel bar, discussing every subject relating to their lives except their physical deformities. That particular topic never came up.

The bar ran out of cranberry juice just after Lucas ordered his fifth glass. "Are you hungry?" he asked. "Wanna go eat someplace?"

"Absolutely and yes," she responded. "Let's forage for food. I refuse to eat at a hotel restaurant that charges thirty bucks for a hamburger."

"Agreed."

A bright, full moon hung in the starry sky. "Look at that moon," Olive said. "It looks like it's being held up by a pair of hands hidden by clouds."

"Yeah, it does," Lucas said. He would've agreed with just about anything Olive said. As he accompanied his new friend down the chilly, bustling street, Lucas was surprised that she made no attempt to hide her webbed hands. She didn't seem to care if anyone noticed them. This buoyed him.

"Delayed luck, that's what I call it," Olive told Lucas.

"Call *what*?" he asked.

"When kids have rotten childhoods, their luck doesn't hit until adulthood. Then they get the luck coming to them *normally* but they also get the residual luck they accrued during those abysmal years, like interest at the bank."

"If that's true," Lucas said with anticipation, "I'm due for a windfall."

The couple found a small, dimly lit French bistro two blocks south of the hotel. The wispy hostess led them to a cozy table that seemed to be waiting for them.

"What I have is called polydactylism," Lucas informed Olive.

"I've heard of that," she said matter-of-factly while perusing the menu. "I have syndactyly. Type 4, which is rare. Do you know what you want to eat?"

"I think I'll have the spinach-and-mushroom crepes, and for dessert, the soufflé au chocolat."

"Must've taken years of French to know *that*!" she said with a grin.

"Three and a half," he responded. "What are *you* in the mood for?" He wondered whether she would order something that didn't necessitate the use of both hands.

"A burger with fries," she said with enthusiasm. "Lots of fries."

"Sounds good." Lucas paused for a moment. "Does anyone else in your family have some kind of uh... ailment?"

"Oh sure," Olive said. "My sister, Hayley, is dyslexic. My cousin, Bart, is diabetic. And my mother is addicted to soap operas."

Lucas couldn't help smiling. He felt that his delayed luck had finally arrived.

The Unlucky

There comes a moment in the life of a severely unlucky person when he or she wonders, with logic and rationality, without sentiment or regret: *Is my life a life worth living?* Pros are measured against cons, happy days are compared to unhappy ones, and a realistic analysis is given to the time remaining: *How much is there? Will it be productive time or miserable months slowly turning into agonizing years? Is it really worth all that suffering for the tiny shred of life that's left?*

Rebecca Ballard was not facing that moment just yet. She did consider herself highly unlucky, but whenever she began to wonder about the intriguing question of life versus death, she quickly came to the conclusion that she was too young to answer it. She had just turned thirty-two.

That proposition always seemed to pop into her head when she was at the home of her older brother and his wife. Fred (owner of a muffin franchise at the local mall) and Lizette (a professor at a community college) were living proof that love conquers all, that the fervent longing one experiences at the beginning of a relationship can last a dozen years. The couple was about to celebrate their twelfth wedding anniversary, and they seemed as enthralled with one another as they did on the day they first met. They never argued, always held hands when strolling down the street, and treated one another in the lovey-dovey way that's usually restricted to couples the week before the wedding.

Rebecca desperately wanted what her sibling had. She was in love with love. Unfortunately, the feeling wasn't mutual. Rebecca's high school romance ended when the boy and his family moved to Saskatchewan. Her one serious post-college relationship ended when, after almost three years, Dirk Singleton came to the conclusion that Rebecca wasn't his soul mate.

Rebecca was thin, but not abnormally so. Still, she always seemed hungry. "You look so hungry," people would tell her. But it wasn't food that she craved. She was famished for love. It was that simple.

Brother and sister were not particularly close during the formative years. Fred had been perfectly content as an only child, and when Rebecca entered the picture shortly after his sixth birthday, he resented her. That resentment lasted until adulthood. When Rebecca was eighteen, their parents were killed in a horrendous automobile accident (they careened off a cliff), leaving the two siblings orphans. But even a traumatic event such as *that* didn't bring them closer together.

It wasn't until Fred met Lizette that he began paying attention to his sister. Lizette had always been devoted to family; not only was she close with her parents but she also spoke to her two brothers every single day. Fred was so in love with Lizette that he wanted her to think *he* was as family oriented as *she* was. He began calling Rebecca on a regular basis, inviting her to cultural events and showing a keen interest in her life. Rebecca was no fool; she understood why Fred was paying so much attention to her. But she *relished* the attention, so she didn't care why it manifested. In fact, she felt indebted to Lizette for giving her the brother she'd always dreamed of having.

At the corporate office where Rebecca worked as an attorney, the guys weren't interested in her. They preferred the more feminine, flirtatious women, many of whom were actively searching for love and marriage; only a few had aspirations of advancing beyond the secretarial pool. (This was St. Louis, Missouri, not New York or Los Angeles.) But Rebecca didn't care; these men repelled her. Focusing on their iPhones during staff meetings was de rigueur as was their relentless pursuit of *more*: more money, more success, more reasons to brag. All Rebecca wanted was a down-to-earth, decent man with down-to-earth, decent goals.

Then an associate named Trevor Hutchison was hired. When Rebecca saw him for the first time, she felt her body temperature rise. She had never felt such heat, not even when she thought she was in love with a landscape artist (appropriately named Leif) whose sculptured cleft made his chin the most-talked-about feature in the neighborhood. It wasn't that Trevor was unusually handsome. He was an inch shorter than Rebecca, his nose was a little too aquiline, and he could rightfully be described as gangly. But there was something about him that made Rebecca melt; he possessed an inexplicable sex appeal.

Trevor's fingers were blissfully bare. (No wedding ring.) Trevor's desk was beautifully devoid of photographs. (No wife, no children.) Trevor had just moved to St. Louis from Little Rock, Arkansas, so he was alone in a brand-new city.

Every Friday evening, the lawyers at the firm went out for drinks to a popular bar one block south of the office. On Trevor's first Friday, Rebecca worked up the courage to stroll down the hallway to Trevor's office, whisking by the offices of colleagues wheeling, dealing, and scanning adult sites on the internet. She peeked in as Trevor perused a document. "Hello, Trevor."

He glanced up, slightly startled. "Hi there," he responded, obviously forgetting Rebecca's name. But the wide grin that gradually took over his face conveyed his pleasure at seeing her standing at the door, and that was more important than remembering a first name.

"A lot of us go out for drinks on Friday after work," she said. "A place called Barney & Clyde's down the street. I hope you'll be joining us."

"Sure, I'll join you," he responded.

"Great," Rebecca replied with a smile, her raspberry daiquiri red-pink lips glowing. The possibility of getting to know this man overshadowed Rebecca's severe aversion to crowds and noise at clubs and bars.

At Barney & Clyde's, the loosening of Trevor's tie and unbuttoning of his shirt only added to the man's sex appeal. Rebecca was breathless, but she didn't want to overwhelm her new colleague, so she played it cool. She spent just enough time with him before deftly maneuvering herself away to chat with someone else. By the end of the evening, the couple had become quite acquainted. "Maybe we could grab a bite after work sometime," Trevor suggested.

"Oh, I'd like that," Rebecca said, deliberately downplaying this magnificent moment, suppressing a powerful urge to scream like a six-year-old who was just promised a trip to the circus. "Maybe early next week?"

"Depending on workload, early next week sounds fine," Trevor said. Rebecca imagined what it would be like to stand next to him and hear him utter the words *I do*.

That weekend, Rebecca was so obsessed with Trevor that it took her a while to realize she hadn't heard from Fred or Lizette in three or four days. This wasn't normal. In fact, it was rather bizarre. When she called, Fred picked up the phone and sounded like a man who had just been brutally punched in the stomach. "What's wrong?" she asked, instantly concerned. When Fred took too long to respond, Rebecca told him she was on her way over.

Under gloomy gray skies, Rebecca drove ten miles faster than the speed limit, blithely unconcerned with traffic safety. She had a gnawing sensation that the news she was about to hear was no trivial matter. She prepared herself for the worst: a catastrophic illness, a pregnancy gone wrong, financial ruin.

Fred appeared even more pathetic in person than he sounded on the phone. His facial hair was growing like an unruly lawn. His rumpled clothes seemed like they'd been worn for a month that contained thirty-one days. The redness in his bewildered eyes, a combination of crimson and magenta, qualified as a new holiday color, and the rest of his face had the pallor of someone who was allergic to the sun. "She left me," he blurted out. "Said she fell in love with someone else."

Those were the very last words Rebecca expected to hear.

"Someone else?" she asked, shocked, bewildered. "Who is he?"

"Some guy she met at the opening of a cheese store.

Funny thing is—I almost went with her that night but at the last minute decided to stay home and watch the game."

"Say Cheese?" Rebecca asked.

"What?"

"Say Cheese. Is that the name of the store?"

"I don't know," he said. "Maybe."

"I think it is. It opened a week or so ago on Lacey Drive next to the shoe repair shop."

"He's one of the owners," Fred added.

"Oh, an owner," Rebecca remarked, surprised. "So, he'll be able to satisfy all her cheese needs."

"He likes to be called a cheese producer. Have you ever heard anything so stupid in your entire life?"

"It's in the top five," she said.

"What does that make *me*?" Fred asked. "A muffin ambassador?"

"Yes. Muffin ambassador. Or diplomat," she suggested. "Do you think there's a chance Lizette will come to her senses?"

"She already moved out," Fred said, his voice cracking. He had to clear his throat before speaking again. "She's living with the hotshot producer."

"The cheese producer."

"Right."

"But she loved you so much, Fred," Rebecca said. "I've never seen a woman treat a man with such devotion." She felt a tremendous rush of tenderness for her brother. It filled her up, gushed inside her, like well water. Comfortably ensconced on the sofa, she lifted her body a few inches in order to put her arms around Fred's shoulders. In this family, at this moment, broken hearts seemed hereditary.

"It doesn't make sense," he said, dumbfounded. "She was never crazy about cheese."

"I've seen her eat her share of Camembert," Rebecca recalled.

"Nah, I think she liked American."

"Nobody likes American," Rebecca explained. "They only eat American when there's no cheddar, Gouda, or Swiss."

"I like a good American cheese sandwich."

"You also like drowning your eggs in ketchup," Rebecca reminded him.

"We're the pair, aren't we?" Fred asked. "A single thirty-two-year-old and her abandoned older brother whose parents killed themselves."

It took a moment for this startling information to sink in. "What do you mean *killed themselves*?" Rebecca asked. "It was an accident."

"Oh, come on. You really think it was an accident? They waited till you were eighteen. Mom didn't want to leave her children until they were old enough. She was always in such a depression, you know that."

"She was moody."

"You don't stay in bed for a week or keep dozens of bottles of sleeping pills at your bedside because you're moody," Fred stated. "She was driving the car, remember?"

"I know she was driving, but.... I don't know if I believe what you're saying." "Makes no difference now," Fred said. "I only bring it up to point out that we've been unlucky from day one, you and me."

"But your luck changed with Lizette," Rebecca

reminded him. "And it'll change again."

"Lizette was a miracle, and miracles only happen once in a lifetime."

"I beg to differ."

"You think I can erase her from my head?" he asked angrily. "You think I can get over her? I'll *never* be over her, not until I breathe my last breath."

Feeling more than slightly dizzy, Rebecca didn't want to say another word. She needed to go home pronto. "Well, if there's anything I can do for you, please let me know."

"There *is* something," Fred said. "Would you throw out all the cheese in the refrigerator? I can't face it."

"Seriously?" she inquired. "You can't face your cheese?"

"That's right, I can't face my cheese. Do you have a problem with that?"

"No, no at all," she said, successfully repressing a giggle. "You don't even want to save a slice or two?"

"Nope," he said. "Destroy it. Massacre it. Shred it all to pieces."

Rebecca rose and made her way to the kitchen for the cheese demolition. The muffin ambassador remained on the sofa, staring into empty space.

On the drive home, Rebecca realized that her notion of a perfect marriage had been destroyed. The picture Fred and Lizette had presented to the world had been false. Inaccurate. A colossal lie. Had Fred begun to take Lizette for granted? Did Lizette always have a roving eye? These were questions Rebecca hoped would be answered. She didn't want to believe that there would be no hope for any other couple on the planet.

But utmost in Rebecca's mind was the unimaginable theory had been introduced by her brother.

That night, she lay in bed and tried to untangle the mess of shock and confusion she felt. She attempted to recall every moment she shared with her mother the week before her tragic demise. These vague memories, the fragmented flashbacks, uncoiled slowly in Rebecca's head. But one recollection emerged with a stunning jolt.

"You're eighteen now," her mother said while she and Rebecca were unpacking groceries in the kitchen. "You can make decisions for yourself. I want you to be wise. And even though your brother's older than you, I want you to keep an eye on him. You're much smarter than he is. Always were."

As thick tears rolled down her cheeks, Rebecca drifted off into a very deep and welcome sleep.

*

From one angle, she looked a bit overdressed and way overdone. From another, she seemed way overdressed and a bit overdone. The pink lace fit-and-flare cocktail dress, though alluring, contained a little too much flare for Rebecca's taste (it didn't seem that way in the store), and the hair, styled beautifully, had much more bounce than usual. In fact, it was bouncing all over the place.

Trevor didn't seem to notice any of it. Nor did he notice the delicate lace choker that adorned his date's dainty neck. "You look nice," he said, and that was all. Five hours of getting ready for a *You look nice*. Not exactly the greatest compliment Rebecca ever received, but she thanked him nonetheless.

Since he was new in town, Rebecca chose the restaurant. She'd been to the Bonefish Grill before, so she knew she could order something that contained few hot spices and nothing that could smell rancid after living in her mouth for an hour or two.

An uncommonly tall waiter in a white shirt and black pants tipped his elongated torso toward Rebecca. She ordered the honey-ginger cedar-plank salmon and Trevor went with the garlic cilantro shrimp. Concerned that she would be preoccupied with all the new information bouncing about in her brain, Rebecca ordered a lemon drop martini. "Could you make it a double please?" she asked.

"Of course," the towering server said. "I'll be back shortly."

Rebecca watched him walk away. "Can he do *anything* shortly?" she whispered after he was out of hearing distance.

"That's funny," Trevor said. "He should really come up with another word."

"*Soon* would suffice," Rebecca suggested. "Or *anon*. Maybe *posthaste*."

"I think *lickety-split* would be good," Trevor offered.

"That's the one!" Rebecca agreed with a laugh. While fiddling with her silverware before the martini arrived, she blurted out the news that her brother's wife just left him after twelve years of what seemed like a perfect marriage.

"I can beat that," Trevor said. "My Aunt Pearl and Uncle Pat were married for thirty-seven years, then they split up when Pearl fell for another gal."

"*Gal?*" Rebecca said. "That must've been a shock."

"Rocked the whole town. Pat only lived another year. Everyone believed he died of a broken heart. I still think it was the cancer that killed him," Trevor said.

"I'd vote for the cancer, too."

"He was a great man, my uncle. Never had a bad word to say about anybody, even when plenty of people around him had bad words to say about *everybody,*"

Trevor shared. "Do you want to hear the startling end to the story?"

"What you told me was pretty darn startling, Trevor. But sure, go ahead."

"A few months after Uncle Pat died, the woman Aunt Pearl left him for was struck by lightning."

"My goodness," Rebecca said. "Did she survive?"

"She couldn't walk or talk, so I don't know if you'd call that surviving."

"A tragedy any way you look at it," Rebecca lamented.

Dinner and drinks were delivered, and all of it was outstanding. Rebecca downed her martini rather quickly and considered ordering another, but she held back. "It was a cheese maker," she said.

"Beg your pardon?"

"My sister-in-law left my brother for a cheese maker," Rebecca stated.

"You mean a cheese producer?" Trevor asked.

"Uh, yes," she responded, floored that he knew the official job title.

"I was always a Gouda guy, but lately I've had a yen for Muenster."

"I see," she said.

"I was at a cheese festival in London, England last year," he shared. "I had no idea there were so many cheeses in the world."

Rebecca suffered through this painful chat about cheese because she felt content, at peace. Trevor was a good, decent guy, a gentleman, and she was enjoying his company.

After sharing a delectable piece of chocolate mousse cake, Trevor took care of the check. "Thanks for a lovely dinner," Rebecca said.

On the drive home, there was no denying the palpable sexual attraction; the car buzzed with electricity. Trevor pulled up to Rebecca's house and turned the engine off. The expected good-night kiss began tentatively and then grew into a hard, hungry one.

Rebecca could taste the now stale garlic from Trevor's shrimp dish, but the thrill of his enthusiastic tongue in her mouth compensated for the rancid taste. The evening ended right then and there, on that perfect note—perfect because they'd gotten along so easily, so naturally, and perfect because, due to the absence of first-date sex, there would be no awkwardness in the office the following Monday morning.

*

When Rebecca hadn't heard from her brother in three days, she called him.

When he didn't pick up the phone, a shudder of fear ripped through her. She felt a kind of dread, a foreboding of some imminent disaster.

She immediately jumped into her car and headed to his house. Behind the wheel, she tried to convince herself that Fred was asleep, shutting out the world now that

Lizette was living with a new man and adding a substantial amount of dairy to her diet.

After parking in the driveway, she emerged from the car and leaned against it. She knew she should race into the house, but an irrational fear held her back. Heart pumping with ferocity, she took a step or two toward the front door. Then she fell to her knees. "I can't," she cried to herself. "I have to go in. But I can't."

She managed to stand up and make it to the door. Her body leaned against it and she called her brother's name. Quietly first, then louder. And louder. She prayed he would hear her and open the door.

The longer she stood there, the more terrified she became. Her right hand rested on the doorknob, but she couldn't move it an inch. Never had she felt anything like this.

She took her left hand and placed it over her right. Somehow she was able to turn the knob.

Unbeknownst to Rebecca, Fred had experienced a profound awakening. With utter logic and rationality, without sentiment or regret, he wondered: *Is my life a life worth living?* Pros were measured against cons, happy days were compared to unhappy ones, and a realistic analysis was given to the time remaining: *How much is there? Will it be productive time or miserable months slowly turning into agonizing years? Is it really worth all that suffering for the tiny shred of life that's left?*

At the age of thirty-eight, Fred Ballard decided his was no longer a life worth living.

Comfort in the Dark

She never admitted this to another human being, but every single morning since she was eight years old, Jeannette McNulty prayed for a power outage.

She wanted it to strike in the early evening. She wanted the lights to be out for at least three hours. She wanted no explanation from the electric company except a simple, "A simple power failure."

Jeannette treasured the moment when television sets died, computers shut down, and refrigerators stopped refrigerating. She relished the very second cell phones and battery-operated radios became the only links to the outside world. Best of all, she cherished the noble march from her fourth-floor apartment to the street below, carefully descending the staircase one step at a time, clutching the railing with one hand and carrying a large flashlight in the other. This trek would never be a solo effort; one or more tenants would undoubtedly join her on the journey with lit candles and jumbo flashlights of their own.

Once she reached the street, Jeannette would mingle with her many neighbors. It was an indelible scene: the residents of this quiet suburb banding together in darkness to become a genuine community. There would be warm smiles, expressions of concern, and a colossal assortment of baked goods courtesy of the town's most popular patisserie, Baking Love.

It was during her third childhood blackout (when she was fourteen) that Jeannette set her sights on becoming an electrical engineer. To be inches from an actual power grid was a thrilling prospect. She could think of no career more satisfying than one devoted to lighting the planet, so it was no surprise that Jeannette's college major was electrical engineering. She graduated with top honors and quickly landed the job of her dreams: Protection and Control Engineer for the electric company. Responsibilities included maintaining power systems, expanding the company's electricity-distribution network, and taking part in preventive maintenance.

On this particular September evening, scores of people poured onto Hicks Avenue having left behind half-eaten dinners, bathtubs half filled with water, homework only partially completed. If it weren't for the anxiety-ridden faces in the crowd, the gathering could have been mistaken for a strawberry festival without the strawberries, a music festival without the music, a farmers' market without the farmers or the market.

Vanessa Penrose lived in the apartment building just north of Jeannette's. The closest of friends, they would always find each other in the crowd. "Net," Jeannette heard from behind.

"Nes," she responded to Vanessa.

"Shouldn't you be trying to get the lights back on?"

"I'm not on emergency duty, so I can stay here and play in the dark."

"How long do you think this damn blackout will last?"

"It could go on for five minutes or five hours." Jeannette took a moment to survey the crowd, nodding to several people, smiling at others. Then her eyes locked on a particular person. "There he is," she said, her voice suddenly soft and soothing.

Vanessa followed Jeannette's gaze. "The Dream," she said.

The Dream was a man of around thirty who lived in the apartment building just south of Jeannette's. She knew nothing about him except that the sight of him made her heart thump louder and faster than usual.

"Why don't you talk to him once and for all?" Vanessa asked, being one who eschewed formality.

"Because that would seem pushy."

"He's standing there alone in the dark. I'd bet my meager savings account he'd like a little company. Now march over there!"

Without hesitation, Jeannette forced herself to follow her friend's command.

As she approached the Dream, her body seemed to throb with adrenaline. When their eyes met, there was a powerful, palpable connection.

"Hello," he said.

A barely audible "Hello" emerged from Jeannette's mouth. Suddenly she was a timid girl of twelve in pigtails.

"Which building do you live in?" he asked. His penetrating blue-gray eyes were like miniature moons illuminating the darkness with soft, celestial light.

"1206."

"I'm 1204," he said.

"Nice building," she said. As soon as the words emerged, Jeannette realized how asinine they were. The building was identical to the building in which *she* lived. Both structures, six stories tall, were part of a larger apartment complex: four buildings in total, all exactly alike. Sturdy, red-brick quadruplets.

"I'm Conor," he said, offering his hand. "One *n*." He had thick, wavy brown hair and a boyishly handsome face.

"I'm Jeannette," she told him, taking his hand in hers. "*Two ns.*"

"Two *ns*? I *envy* that," he said with a sly grin. "Sorry to meet under these circumstances."

"You should look on the bright side!" she exclaimed a bit too cheerfully.

"There's a bright side in the dark?" he asked. "Where?"

"Well, look at this as an opportunity to get to know your neighbors."

"All right," he acknowledged with a tentative smile. "But it might be hard. I've had some bad experiences in blackouts."

"Oh," Jeannette said, taken aback. "Sorry to hear that."

"I'll tell you about them sometime." Extremely eager to change the subject, he asked, "What's interesting about you that I should know?"

"Well," she hesitated. "You go first."

"All right." He regaled her with stories about growing with two lesbian mothers, playing the trumpet as a teenager, and currently working for a top accounting firm.

"Why aren't you a world-famous trumpet player?" she boldly inquired.

"I didn't love it enough," he explained. "You have to live and breathe it, and I just didn't. Do *you* live and breathe anything?"

"Yes, I do," she said. "But I'll tell you about that another time."

"Why don't you tell me at dinner one night?" he asked.

"Sounds like a plan," she said, thrilled beyond belief.

After exchanging phone numbers through their mobile devices, Conor searched Jeannette's face as if seeking permission to make some kind of confession.

"What's wrong?" she asked.

Conor hesitated. "I should probably tell you why I hate blackouts."

Jeannette didn't want anything to tarnish her warm and fuzzy feelings about power failures, especially the current one, but she knew she had to listen with empathy. "Tell me," she said, bracing herself.

"When I was twelve, there was a power failure," he somberly told her. "My mom was a doctor at the hospital. When the electricity went out, one of the emergency back-up generators failed, so the machines stopped working. My mom lost two of her patients. One was just a kid, around five or six."

The information hit Jeannette like a thunderbolt. "That's horrendous," she said. "Back-up systems are supposed to work. I've never heard of one that didn't function properly."

"Well, this one didn't." He took a long breath and peered pensively into the darkness. "There's more," he said.

The last thing Jeannette wanted to hear was another nightmare blackout saga, but she was Conor's audience of one, and she had no choice. "I'm listening," she told him.

"While that was happening, my other mom at home wanted to get candles from the basement, so she started walking down the long wooden staircase. It was pitch black and she lost her balance. Fell all the way down. Hit her head on the concrete floor," he said. "She died."

Jeannette and Conor were silent for a few moments, the horror of this message infiltrating the space around them like poison from a chemical weapon; there was nothing left to breathe.

"It was a long time ago," Conor said, his voice congested with pain. "Whenever there's a power outage, I still worry that someone might get hurt."

This harrowing, heartbreaking information echoed through eighteen years of Jeannette's life, obliterating every bit of joy she ever felt about power failures. In a matter of seconds, the entire tapestry of her life immutably changed. Even the thrill of meeting Conor faded like smoke dissipating into thin air.

"Let's just hope the lights will be on soon," he said.

"The lights will be on before midnight," she announced with authority, the professional part of her emerging from the shadows.

"How do you know that?" Conor asked.

"I work at the electric company," Jeannette said, trying her best to conceal the fact that her world had just fallen spectacularly to pieces. "We can always fix a malfunction within a few hours."

"You work at the electric company?" he asked, twisting his face into a question mark.

"I do. I work at the electric company," she repeated.

"Then you must take this power outage pretty seriously."

"I live and breathe it," she shared, feeling dizzy and sick, the way she felt when forced to sit in a backwards-facing seat on a train. Suddenly, an ear-splitting cry of "Help!" rattled the crowd.

Just yards away from Jeannette and Conor, septuagenarian Liam Donnelly, a kind and well-liked neighbor, had collapsed to the ground. "He was clutching his arm!" his wife screamed.

"He's having a heart attack!" some man shouted. "Call 911!"

"Give him space!" a neighbor called out.

A young woman quickly kneeled down and began to administer CPR. "Is there a doctor here?" his wife shrieked. "We need a doctor!"

Within minutes, an ambulance could be heard approaching. But instead of appearing rapidly, the ambulance couldn't get near Mr. Donnelly because of the pedestrians pouring onto the street. The siren seemed to become louder and louder as if shouting to the crowd to move out of the way. "Let the ambulance through!" Jeannette screamed. "Get out of the way!" But the people were slow to disperse, and it seemed to be taking forever for the car to get to the patient, clinging to life.

"Move away!" Jeannette continued to shriek.

"Oh my God!" a woman shouted.

"He's dying!" someone else yelled.

Chaos ensued as the ambulance crept closer and closer.

Jeannette trudged through the crowd, completely forgetting about Conor and feeling like an enemy of the people. If she had thought of the potential danger beforehand, she wouldn't have engineered the outage, and she wouldn't have found herself in the eye of this emotional tornado. She found it strange and distressing to walk among the living when she might be causing someone's death that very moment. She wanted to apologize to every single person she passed.

The plan was so simple that it bordered on humorous, Jeannette had initially thought. A surreptitious entry into a computer to program a power outage, and the lights went out on schedule. The power would be restored just before midnight, perhaps sooner if the technicians were savvy enough.

Not only was this action morally reprehensible, it was completely against company policy. When Jeannette first landed the job, she attended a series of meetings about the procedures, regulations and values of the electric company. There was a document she was required to sign promising she would uphold the company's strict, scrupulous standards to the best of her ability. If this blackout was ever traced to her, she would be fired on the spot.

The night air had turned cold. The din of the crowd was deafening. The streets, wrapped in darkness, were devoid of camaraderie, completely barren of the warmth and friendship Jeannette had loved about blackouts.

Jeannette raced to the parking lot behind her building. She didn't plan, she didn't think. Her body just moved and she followed.

She climbed into the driver's seat of her dark-blue sedan, started the engine, and zoomed away.

There weren't many cars on the road, but the hordes of people on the street caused frustrating delays. Dedicated police officers, standing in the middle of chaotic intersections, did their best to direct traffic.

Then the clouds opened up, and rain cascaded down on the darkness. Within minutes, a light drizzle turned into a deluge, and Jeannette's windshield wipers could barely keep up with the heavy downpour of drops. She pictured her neighbors, hundreds of them, rushing indoors to fetch raincoats and umbrellas. She envisioned screaming, crying, pandemonium. She saw accidents happening. She wondered what her ultimate punishment might be.

For the very first time in her life, the notion of a blackout terrified her.

Driving as quickly as the traffic and weather allowed, Jeannette found her way to the electric company. She pulled into the parking lot and screeched to a halt, almost slamming into one of the two gigantic dumpsters that squatted near the entrance. Then she raced into the building, becoming drenched in the process. Even though she wasn't officially on duty, she would do whatever she could to restore power as promptly and efficiently as possible.

The Eternal Rinse Cycle

"Miss Varnish," the police officer with the movie-star looks said, "you were found with a smoking revolver standing over the victim, who happened to be your lover, and you're telling me you're innocent?"

"Sometimes you do what you're not supposed to do but it's the *right* thing to do, even if there's some nutty law against it," Ravina Varnish replied.

The suspect appeared rumpled and disheveled. Still, a sensual radiance oozed from her, as if her mess of an appearance was the result of mad, raucous monkey love. Officer Calvin Clout couldn't help falling under her spell. Strangely entranced by her blood-red lips, blood-red nails, and the dried blood on her forearm that was salmon pink, he found himself sweating profusely and hoping the perspiration was being absorbed by his tight white T-shirt. "There's no getting around the fact that you committed murder," he stated. "Is that correct?"

"Look, I may have *socialized* with murderers, *worked* with murderers, even *slept* with a dozen or two, but you are *not* the company you keep."

"May I remind you, Miss Varnish, that murder is murder, punishable by decades in a dark, dank penitentiary."

"I don't have decades, Detective," she pleaded. "I'm planning to spend Christmas in Honolulu, Machu Picchu, and the People's Republic of Bangladesh."

"I hope your tickets are refundable," he said, loosening his royal-blue necktie. "We're discussing the murder of a human being here."

"You don't get it, do you? Moose McGill wasn't human. He was barbaric and depraved, heartless and heinous. And on *bad* days he was worse. Do you happen to have a decorative pillow? This chair is brutal on my butt."

"Uh no, I don't," he told her.

"So, what happens when you discover the straight dope, huh?" Ravina asked. "*You* get a promotion and *I'm* thrown in the slammer?"

"Not necessarily," Calvin explained, examining Ravina's face as if searching for some clue to her strange, disturbing psyche. She held perfectly still, allowing him to look. She *liked* being admired. "But I need to know everything there is to know about you."

"Such as?" she inquired.

"Let's start at the start. What was your childhood like?"

"Small-town hell," Ravina began. "Mother was manic, sister depressed. Father had four other wives in three other counties, not to mention two other kids with one more on the way. There was a state prison nearby, so we assumed any burly stranger on the street was an escaped convict who would follow us home and kill us in our sleep."

"Sounds like a charmed childhood," he remarked. "Please continue, if you will."

"My breasts were titanic for a girl of fifteen, so I was a pariah to everyone except Federal Express delivery men and the Detroit chapter of the Boy Scouts of America. I had to cut loose," Ravina explained, "so I skipped town as soon as I saved enough money from babysitting the neighborhood brats. Hopped a midnight train to Athens, Georgia because it sounded romantic. But the place was stifling, and the accent revolted me. Then I headed north by northwest."

"Where exactly?" Clout inquired.

"Soddy-Daisy, Tennessee; the Carolinas; Baltimore, MD. I met an MD in MD. I would've *killed* to be a doctor's wife, but this quack was too quirky, even for me."

The officer took copious notes on his large yellow pad. "Let's jump ahead to present day. What do you do in your leisure time?"

Discussing her leisure activities wasn't something Ravina was keen on doing at the moment, but she realized she had little choice. "I play the lute, the flute, and the French horn," she blandly stated, as if reading a laundry list. "I write to the Menendez brothers once a month. I do the shopping for a paraplegic paralegal. She has no trouble getting to work, but *you* try getting to the front of a crowded deli counter on crutches, Calvin Clout."

The officer was perplexed. "Why did the good-natured citizen you just described allow herself to get involved with a mobster like Moose McGill?"

"He may've been a mobster, but he was charming and seductive, too. He could coax a kid out of a candy bar," she explained. "I'll bet *you* know how to seduce a dame, Detective."

"Why do you say that?" he asked, leaning against his dark wooden desk. His heart was beginning to race.

"Because of your broad shoulders and blond hair, your

muscular thighs and jumbo stapler. You're the boy next door all grown up and eager to taste life, aren't you?"

"If I am," Calvin replied, "you're the *girl* next door all *beaten* up and tired of the life you've tasted." He unbuttoned the top few buttons of his white oxford shirt. "You see, I would treat a dame with respect. I wouldn't force her to tattoo my initials on her butt. I wouldn't give pet names to each of her breasts. I wouldn't force her to pleasure me in a bowling alley just because it's my birthday. I don't *have* demented thoughts like that, the kind Moose McGill had."

Ravina seemed bewildered. "He didn't have thoughts like that."

"Did you know his past was peppered with pandering, perjury, battery, burglary, tax evasion, embezzlement, and manslaughter?"

"I knew every rotten thing there was to *know* about him," she said. "Do you happen to have an amphetamine? I'm dog-tired."

"Uh, no I don't," the officer informed her. Then, dramatically changing the subject, he asked, "Why did you blast Moose McGill away?"

"Because he was about to blast *me* away," Ravina responded with conviction. "It was self-defense, I tell you, defense of the living, breathing human being with the big boobs sitting right here."

"So you say," he said. "Where did you first meet McGill?"

"At my Laundromat, Ravina's Rinse Cycle, corner of Jaundice and Shank."

"And how'd you get involved with a Laundromat?"

Ravina took a deep, mordant breath. "I was a

receptionist at The Sunshine Institute for the Criminally Insane. One Saturday morning, Mr. Kasper Leek was visiting his wife, Martha, who kidnapped two of his mistresses before dehydrating them to death. He smelled so clean and fresh, like a sheet of fabric softener. Turns out he owned a string of Laundromats. Anyway, Leek took a liking to me, so we went to lunch at Ruth's Chris Cafeteria for the Criminally Insane on the institute grounds. Over a bowl of cream of crab soup and a rare, juicy sirloin, he offered me the manager gig at Coin Laundry. I grabbed it. Decided to take that rotting, stinking dump, change its name to Ravina's Rinse Cycle, and turn it into a showplace. Twenty shining washers, sixteen state-of-the-art dryers. I got such a kick strolling up and down the aisles, watching dingy whites become snowy bright, checking out the different kinds of underwear in people's loads."

"Sounds like loads of fun."

"It was more than just fun, Officer. It was a slice of heaven on earth," Ravina marveled. "I played modern jazz, hired local vocalists, even had a bulletin board where people tacked up index cards looking for work, apartments for rent or deviant sex partners. The place was a beehive of activity, buzzing with life. Some thought of it as a community center where you could be yourself and air your dirty laundry, too. And on the first Saturday night of spring, I threw a big, blowout party to end all parties. That's where I made the regrettable acquaintance of Moose McGill."

"Tell me more about meeting McGill. I need details."

Ravina heaved a heavy sigh, then recalled a day three months earlier. "It was the second night of spring after a frightfully frigid winter. Three blizzards and four monsoons in February alone. The snow banks froze into gray barricades as impenetrable as anything built by the Bolsheviks during the Russian Revolution. Yes, it was the night of my grand and glorious soiree. It was also the night of the fire, the big blaze at the greenhouse of my dear friend Dolores Miranda. I was all dolled up, dressed in a buttercup yellow, scoop-neck silk number, classy but casual, the kind of outfit Gwyneth Paltrow might wear to a Pap smear..."

Three Months Earlier

It was a dry, gray April evening. The air outside Ravina's Rinse Cycle smelled of ash due to the blaze that burned Dolores's Glorious Greens to the ground six blocks southeast, on the corner of Glen Oaks Lane and Vendetta. Dolores McGill Miranda owned the place, and whispers spread with the wind: Had she been growing more than daffodils and bougainvillea?

Ravina proudly stood next to washer number one to greet her guests as they arrived.

Every heavyweight in town showed up to the shindig. The mayor's russet-haired mistress Camille Crookshank entered with her bulky half-brother Brigham.

Sex surrogate Rochelle Fervor arrived with her bulimic half-sister Louise. Underground entertainer Beneatha Sink waltzed through the door in full dazzling drag, carrying a laundry basket filled to the brim. "I hope you don't mind. I brought a load of whites."

"Of course not," Ravina said. "Throw it in number nine."

"Thanks, doll."

The undisputed king of pimps Nicky Zetts escorted his latest squeeze Caressa Schildkraut, a nubile new hooker in the 'hood. Airline heiress Bitsy Woo flew through the door with swarthy pilot Sankara Zheng on her arm. "Bitsy, is that a new 'do?" Ravina asked.

"You betcha!" she chirped. "You like?"

"I *love*!" Ravina gushed. "Makes you look like renowned American soprano Renee Fleming."

"That's what *I* told her," Sankara said.

Ravina was thrilled to see the three-times-married Amber Schifflet Mooney Bupkiss Sopp enter the Laundromat wearing her silk organza wedding dress. "Why the outfit?" Ravina inquired.

"Who says you can only wear a wedding gown three times?" she quipped.

"Good thinking. Where's the chubby hubby?"

"I threw him the hell out," she said. "Caught him cheating with some Moroccan tramp."

Taxi cab mogul Vince Fraggle arrived with his statuesque wife Solange Fournier-Fraggle. Podiatrist Arturo DiBenedetti entered with Athena Thorpe, a platinum blonde he had recently cured of a bunionette on her big toe. Shooting range instructor Guy Shafranski brought his sultry ammunitions expert Ursula Embers. Professional witness Bingo Frost made a solo entrance in an off-the-shoulder lace-trimmed dress that showcased her lithe figure. "My word," Ravina said, "you look stunning."

"Thanks, doll," Bingo said. "It's the hula hoop. Took two inches off my waist."

An abundant flow of guests, all of whom seemed to be

presenting themselves onstage, arrived as rhythm and blues blended softly with the clamor. A platter of pepperoni pinwheels sat atop washer number four and a bowl of butternut squash wontons on number five. There were veal shanks, lamb pizzettes, cod cakes, and ricotta fritters to nibble on too, not to mention sponge cakes soaked in Grand Marnier. Guests chewed and sipped as they indulged in polite party conversation.

"As a professional witness, what exactly do you do?" Caressa asked Bingo.

"Well, after I'm hired, the client tells me what he was charged with and what he wants me to say on the stand. So I research the hell out of the case and come up with the most solid alibi," Bingo explained. "On the day of the trial, I dress like a dimwitted White House Press Secretary: designer suit, pearl necklace, patent leather pumps. When it's time, I hold my head high and take the witness stand. Then I swear I saw *this*, swear I saw *that*, whatever the client needs me to say under oath."

"Amazing," Caressa remarked. "Does it pay well?"

Bingo held up a glistening five karat bauble on her left ring finger. "A bonus from my last boss. But that's only if I get them off," she said, her curious eyes scanning the room.

"I get my clients off all the time and no one gives me presents like that," Caressa confessed with disappointment.

Just then, Lysistrata Goot stepped into the party and all eyes flew to her scintillating outfit, particularly her smoked salmon blouse. Smoked salmon wasn't merely the *color* of the top; it was the material: 100% smoked fish. To offset the blouse, she wore a black sequined, see-through, pajama-style pair of pants. On her head was a two-foot headpiece created with more than eight hundred rooster feathers. Ravina instantly rushed over.

"Lysistrata, my love," the hostess gushed, "if there was a Most Original Outfit contest tonight, you would win hands-down."

"Thank you, sweetness," Lysistrata said. "I so appreciate that."

Close to nine, he arrived. Moose McGill exploded through the front door like a mudslide. With a face that seemed mauled by a Mack truck, fingernails lined with grease, and clothes that hadn't been washed in weeks, he resembled a creature from the Neanderthal era. Still, he managed to exude a boyish charm. "Do you have an invitation?" Ravina asked. "Because I don't know who the hell you are."

"I'm a guest of Dolores McGill Miranda," he responded defiantly. "I'm her baby brother Moose."

"Dolores hasn't arrived yet," she stated with attitude.

"That's because her beloved greenhouse burned down."

"Well, you can wait for her outside."

"Listen, sweetheart," Moose said, so wound up he seemed capable of exploding, "I have a history of bronchial asthma, asthmatic bronchitis, whooping cough, and croup. You really gonna make me wait out there and catch emphysema?"

"I'll get you a gas mask," Ravina offered.

"I'd really like to stay inside."

Ravina gave him a quick once-over. "All right, fine," she conceded. "I like your mustard-colored shirt."

"Thanks."

"Matches your teeth."

"Where's the vodka?" Moose asked.

"Washer number six," Ravina told him. "Ice is in seven. Open bar in the back."

The hostess kept her eyes on the sturdy round butt of her unexpected arrival as he disappeared into the crowd.

An hour later, when lively, vibrant salsa music inspired a dozen couples to shake it up on the dance floor, the front door opened and Dolores McGill Miranda rushed over to Ravina. "My greenhouse is gone," she sobbed in a state of quasi-hysteria. "Every succulent shrub I nurtured, every African violet, every frigging ficus is nothing but ashes."

"Oh, sweetie," Ravina said, "I'm so sorry. Do you think it was an accident?"

"Accident my foot!" Dolores snapped. "Babs DuBarry did it. Is she in the house?"

"No, but she did RSVP so I expect to see her face at some point." Ravina couldn't help noticing Dolores's long painted fingernails, each with a colorful design resembling a stained glass window.

"You like them?" Dolores asked, allowing her hand to float in midair. "Instead of going to church on Sunday, I look at my nails and it's like I'm there."

"Well, you know who's *here*? Your brother."

"Moose?"

"That's right. Moose."

"That loser's supposed to be at a rehab facility in Roanoke."

"Rehab for what?"

"You name it: drinking, drugs, smoking, sex, guns, lunch meat, glue, gambling, graft."

Just then, the man of the moment ran up to the ladies. "Dolores! Are you OK?" Moose asked.

"My baby brother," she said with disgust. "Yeah, I'm jubilant. Rollicking in my Prada espadrilles. Why aren't you in rehab?"

"Because those people don't know how to have any fun," he reported.

"I don't think fun is the objective, you thick-skulled moron," Dolores barked.

"Look, I heard about your greenhouse," Moose said, "and I'll get the one who did it, I swear."

"You're all talk," Dolores told him.

"Can't you be nice to me?" he asked. "I'm your only blood relative."

"I'll remember that when I need a transfusion," she said. "Did you meet Ravina?"

"Sure did," he said with a lusty, self-satisfied grin. "This gorgeous doll greeted me when I walked in."

"Stay away from this one," Dolores quietly warned Ravina. "The man is truly disturbed. Just *look* at the way he's dressed."

"Hey," Moose said in his defense. "You can't judge a book by its cover."

"A book?" she exclaimed with a chuckle. "With your brains it would be more like a pamphlet."

"Dolores, I'll make a sacred promise to you. Whoever's responsible for the destruction of your nursery will pay through their lying nose. I'll see to that!"

"So you're a hero all of a sudden. I won't hold my breath," she said. "I need a cocktail."

Dolores ambled away, leaving Ravina and Moose alone. "How long have you known my sister?" he asked.

"Long time. She represented my friend Conji Fox in a felony case."

"Conji?"

"Short for Conjugal," Ravina said.

"Did she win?" he asked.

"You don't know your sister too well, do you? Dolores wins every case she tries."

"I guess she got the brains in the family and I got the looks."

"Somebody forgot to give you a mirror, Mr. Moose McGill."

Surrounded by a circle of four strapping thugs in black Versace suits, Babs DuBarry slipped into the party. With her alabaster skin, goth eyes, mocha lips, wide hips, and shock of flaming-orange-red hair with black braid cascading down her back, she was a stunning, odd-looking creature. A combination of Irish peasant girl and Apache princess, even her unusually crooked teeth seemed that way on purpose, an ivory Stonehenge. In order to maintain a low profile, she and her posse planted themselves in the rear, next to dryer number nineteen.

Dolores could hardly believe Babs showed up. "Well, *there's* the one who did it, Moose," Dolores said, sipping a Singapore Sling. "Babs DuBarry, with her henchmen in tow."

"I wonder if she'll have the gall to look you in the eye," Ravina said.

Within ninety seconds, Ravina got her answer. Slowly and defiantly, Babs approached her nemesis. "Dolores, my goodness. You look somewhat presentable, considering the unfortunate circumstances. If *my* place of business accidentally perished in a colossal blaze, I'd be medicated and supine."

"Aren't you *usually* that way?" Dolores replied.

"You've always had an almost-clever wit," Babs croaked. "My heart, my soul, my guts go out to you."

"Keep your guts to yourself, will you?" Dolores growled. "Your maudlin expressions of sympathy are as authentic as supermarket sushi. Why don't you take your false teeth out and give your gums a rest?"

"You're simply jealous of me because I can pass for thirty-five."

"Where, at the Braille Institute?" Dolores quipped. "How dare you display yourself in public after what you pulled tonight?"

"You don't think *yours truly* had anything to do with the destruction of your little plant store, do you?" Babs inquired. "You must cease and desist spreading that erroneous rumor, that falsehood, that tall, towering, lie-infested tale."

"Your method for escaping failure is to burn down the competition," Dolores ranted. "If you think you can have a monopoly on the growth of certain substances, you know nothing about the world of business. Competition is healthy."

"I don't enjoy competing with amateurs, my bovine beauty. I prefer to wipe them out before they make even the slightest dent in my bottom line."

Suddenly sensual tango music filled the room. Several couples took to the dance floor, then Babs grabbed one of her henchmen. Moving like elegant cougars, their staccato moves and dramatic head-snaps dazzled the onlookers. At a crucial moment in the dance when Babs was kneeling on the ground, Moose grabbed his sister and pulled her to the center of the room. Babs seems horrified.

Moose maintained a solid grip. This Danse Macabre continued with stalking, slithery movements until Dolores literally shoved him off the floor with force. Then the two women went at each other, venom spewing. With a series of quick foot-flicks, Dolores took charge and wowed their onlookers, who whooped and cheered. But then, Babs performed a truly impressive gancho by hooking one leg around Dolores's body and rendering the woman helpless. The crowd went crazy.

When the music ended, the women instantly trotted off to their separate corners like boxers when the bell sounds.

"She may be a sadistic, cold-blooded, foul-mouthed fire starter," Ravina said to Moose, "but that bitch can sure tango."

The party was a huge success. Ravina saw to it that every one of her guests had a memorable time. She even managed to play matchmaker, hooking up Camille Crookshank's chunky half-brother with Rochelle Fervor's starving half-sister. She did the same for the three-times-married Amber Schifflet Mooney Bupkiss Sopp and the newly single Montserrat Crescendo, a smoldering but shady import king who had recently lost his wife, Jill. (She didn't die. He literally lost her at Disney World on a jam-packed Sunday afternoon.)

The moment the last guest left the premises, Moose pinned Ravina to washer number one and kissed her with hunger. She tasted tobacco and vodka and a little veal in his mouth, but she didn't care. The kiss became so intense that the couple spent the next six minutes making mad, passionate love on top of washing machines number two, three, and four.

This was the start of a tumultuous affair. For two idyllic, euphoric weeks, Moose spent every evening at the Laundromat, washing his greasy garments and gazing at his ladylove. Ravina was mystified by her attraction to this lug, but she didn't resist. Moose seemed genuinely interested in hearing about Ravina's tormented childhood and abandoned pipe dreams. He was astonished to learn that she'd even given birth to a baby.

"Really?" Moose asked. "You hatched a kid?"

Suddenly Ravina was filled with emotion. "I'll say this one time, not two: Tina's Three Musketeer Lounge. Fourth of July. Five years ago. Six guys walked in at seven p.m. Ate all the pretzels. By nine, I fell for the tennis pro. Next thing I knew I was knocked up. The following March I gave birth to a bouncing baby girl. Eleven pounds."

"So where are you hiding her?" Moose asked.

"Who do I look like—Miep Gies? I'm not hiding anybody!" Ravina exclaimed. "She deserved a decent life, so I handed her over to a frizzy-haired dame from the Shoshanna Schwab Adoption Agency. My precious girl is with a family of linguistics professors at the University of Wisconsin at Stout. Probably speaks three languages by now."

"You did a noble thing, Ravina Varnish."

"Thank you, Moose."

Four nights after that heartfelt confession, Moose marched into the Laundromat wheeling a jumbo, metal-sided suitcase. "What's in that thing?" Ravina asked with curiosity.

In his badly stained, wrinkled clothes, he gently sat on the large piece of luggage. "Nice, strong case, huh?"

"Yeah, very nice," she said. "What's in it?"

"You'll never guess."

"I wasn't planning to, Moose," Ravina said. "Just tell me what's inside. You going on a trip?"

"I ain't leaving your side, baby," he said with a sly grin.

"Are *we* going on a trip?" she inquired with excitement. "Are you taking me to Branson or Bermuda?"

"No, baby. I'll take you on a trip sometime, but not *this* week."

"Then what's the suitcase for?" she asked, becoming impatient.

"The suitcase is part of a master plan," he said. "Probably the most brilliant plan anyone ever came up with."

"So tell me already."

"You're gonna think I'm a genius," he boasted.

"OK, genius. I'm listening."

Moose took a long, deep, contented breath. "The cops always find the corpse," he explained. "You could dump it in the river or bury it in a ditch, they'll discover it."

"What corpse? What the heck are you babbling about?" Ravina asked.

"One place they'd never look is inside a washing machine if it was in the middle of a rinse cycle. That's why I brought the body of Babs DuBarry with me."

"You're sitting on the body of Babs DuBarry?" Ravina asked, horrified.

"Yeah, but don't worry, it's hacked up into little chunks, like squares of cheese," he said, avoiding eye contact. "The kind you eat with a toothpick."

"Right," she said with revulsion.

"Now listen, doll," he said. "You can program one of your machines to run continuously, right?"

"Yeah. So?"

"So that's what I want you to do," Moose told her.

"Are you kidding me?" she asked. "You want me to stuff the body of Babs DuBarry into one of my washing machines?"

"Genius idea, huh?"

"You are an animal," Ravina barked. "A despicable creature who belongs behind bars. Not in a prison. In a zoo!"

Moose told her some of the heinous acts Babs DuBarry had performed, like smothering her own mother and torturing a ten-year-old girl who knew too much. But that didn't make the slightest dent in Ravina's disgust.

"I promised my sister I'd seek revenge," Moose explained, "and I did."

"Do you actually think Dolores would approve of your method of revenge?" Ravina shouted.

"What's the difference? Right now I gotta find a place to hide this human flesh and bone, and you have to agree that one of your washing machines is the most convenient spot."

"Absolutely not."

Moose's jaw tightened. "Ravina, you gotta help me. I don't know where else to put this except in a washing machine or maybe under your mattress."

"My mattress?" she squealed.

"Yeah," he threatened. "Your mattress."

Against her better judgment, Ravina gave Moose access to washing machine number six. "Heaven, forgive me," she muttered. She promised to make sure it was always running which meant that it would always be locked. That, Ravina hoped, would be the end of that.

Every single morning for the following week, Ravina awakened with a sick feeling in her stomach, knowing her customers would be washing their clothes near a cut up cadaver in the rinse cycle. Luckily, the detergent and bleach disguised the foul smell that might have been emanating from washer number six.

Exactly eight nights after wheeling the body of Babs DuBarry into the Laundromat, Moose came strolling in with the same metal suitcase. This time, the chopped body of Montserrat Crescendo was stuffed between its solid silver sides, and Moose requested the unlimited use of washing machine number seven. Ravina asked why he butchered the import king, but the anger bubbled so intensely in her veins that she couldn't follow his cockamamie explanation.

"You're a disgrace to the human race," Ravina told him. "I refuse to turn my respectable place of business into a depository for cut up cadavers. I want you to clean out washer number six, and never step foot in this Laundromat again."

"Too late to play Snow White," he groaned, throwing his lit cigarette on the floor with frustration. "You're an accessory, doll. A great big accessory." He warned Ravina that if she didn't cooperate, she'd be chopped into small pieces and stuffed into washer number eight with a cup of Tide and a capful of bleach. "Is that the way you want to spend eternity?" he asked. "In a rinse cycle?"

Ravina's head began to spin. She was afraid she might pass out, so she sat down and shut her exceedingly tired eyes. She had always imagined growing old with a close companion by her side. Now she had to imagine growing old in a basin of suds.

"Come on, baby," Moose said. "This is the reality. And as we all know, reality bites."

"I bite back."

"Reality's teeth are bigger than yours. Look, once we take care of this, I'll plan a vacation for us. Any place you wanna go. Niagara Falls? Miami Beach? Atlantic City?"

"At this moment, travel is the last thing on my mind, Moose."

"What *is* on your mind?"

"What to do with the contents in that suitcase."

"I knew you'd see the light, baby," Moose said.

What Ravina really saw was the dark—the dark, ugly face of evil, a monster who chopped people into bits like ground beef, a killer who casually wheeled around a corpse in a piece of luggage like it was his wardrobe for a weekend getaway to Antigua. She feared that restless spirits would begin to swoosh their way up and down the aisle that separated the washing machines from the dryers. She wondered if some of her psychic customers (of which there were several) would sense something evil in the air, take their dirty clothing to Washing Wells Laundry on Verminette Boulevard, and eventually force Ravina to declare bankruptcy.

And Ravina Varnish, charming hostess, astute businesswoman, and laundress extraordinaire, saw no way out. Except one.

Back to the Present

"So, it was a form of self-defense," Officer Calvin

Clout said to Ravina, greatly relieved to learn that the bewitching woman in his presence wasn't a cold-blooded killer.

"A combination of self-defense and trying to keep my business afloat," she explained.

"What you need is a good lawyer," he suggested.

"I know that. I want Dolores McGill Miranda."

"You want a botanist to represent you?" Calvin asked.

"Dolores has two careers," Ravina explained, "like actors who become restaurateurs. She runs a successful law practice *and* she owned Dolores's Glorious Greens."

"In any case, I don't think it would be proper for the sister of the deceased to represent you."

"I don't care about proper," Ravina barked.

"You never *did*, did you?" the officer commented. "I'm beginning to see how you tick."

"Tick, huh?" she asked. "I think you're strangely intoxicated by me."

"Don't turn the tables, Miss Varnish."

"I know when a guy is intoxicated, and I know when he's intoxicated by *me*. You, Officer Clout, are intoxicated by *me*. Admit it."

"You think I'm playing games here?" he pointedly asked. "You think I'll fall for your seductive charms like some thick-headed thug off the street?"

"So, you think I have seductive charms?" she coyly inquired.

"I didn't say that."

"Sure you did."

"Well, even if I *suggested* you might have certain uh... charms, that doesn't mean I'd fall for 'em."

"Ha!" Ravina balked. "You already have."

"Let's just say, purely for argument's sake, that I *have*. Do you think that changes anything?"

"Changes everything," Ravina insisted. "But I've known phonies like you. All you want is a *little* danger. You stick it in your mouth, swish it around, then spit it out because it tastes like bad tiramisu."

"You've had bad tiramisu?" he asked.

"I've had bad *everything*," she confessed. "Let me know when you're ready to shake your life up, when you're ready for some *real* danger."

It was time for Ravina to be taken to county jail. "We'll definitely meet again, Miss Varnish," Calvin said. "I'll see to that."

With sleepy seductiveness, Ravina approached the officer and brought her lips as close to his as possible without touching them. Calvin felt weak, disoriented. Lunging in for a deep kiss was as tempting as reading a diary that was left open by accident or devouring what was left of a half-eaten chocolate birthday cake. But Ravina didn't allow it to happen. She simply turned and sauntered out.

The very next day, attorney Dolores McGill Miranda conferred with her new client. "If I'd known what my demented brother was up to, I would've ripped his heart out with my bare hands."

"Do you think we have a shot in hell for acquittal?" Ravina asked.

"You bet your shapely ass we do!" she exclaimed.

Ravina felt confident. She was glad her future was in this able woman's religiously manicured hands.

Bingo Frost offered her services as a professional witness. This was a tremendously appealing scenario for

Ravina. Under oath, Bingo would say that she witnessed Moose threaten Ravina with her life. Under oath, Bingo would swear that Ravina acted out of self-defense, that she shot Moose because he was just about to shoot *her*. But after seriously mulling the offer, Ravina decided to go it alone. She would win this case on her own merit or rot in jail for the rest of her life.

The days leading up to the trial resembled a circus. Dozens of reporters gathered outside Ravina's Rinse Cycle. Some pretended they had dirty laundry to wash in order to get inside and take a photo with the accused murderess. The regular customers felt special, as if their Laundromat of choice was the most popular destination in the city. Reporters from several international publications were present: *The Sydney Morning Herald*, *The Times of India*, *Suddeuttsche Zeitung*, *Komsomolskaya Pravda*, and *The Yangtse Evening Post*. In fact, Ravina had become such a celebrity in Japan that an Asian liquor company offered to fly her first class to Toyko to be featured in a new advertising campaign. But the in-demand charmer was forbidden to leave her native land, so she had to turn the lucrative offer down.

Ravina's opposing counsel, a portly, bearded, smug Mr. Simon Bugg had a field day.

"Ravina Varnish is no angel," he stated to the court. "She's the kind of gal who takes pleasure in breaking rules, laws, hearts, wind, bread, you name it. The bitch likes *breaking* things, and she takes joy in killing those who stand in her way. But she's an extremely unique subject, and here's why: The destruction of human life happens to be an inherited trait in the Varnish family, as I will prove today. The defendant has volunteered to take the stand because she'd like to tell her sordid story in her own sordid words. Security, be on alert—there's no telling what could take place. Now, will Miss Ravina Varnish please get off her rump and take center stage?"

Ravina stood up, and with her head held high, she took the stand.

"Would you state your full name for the court, please?" Bugg asked.

"Ravina Regina Varnish."

After Ravina swore to tell the truth and nothing but the truth, Bugg began his questioning. "Can you tell the court the identity of Viveca Venetia Varnish?"

"She was my tormented, talented mother."

"Why would you call her tormented?"

"Because Daddy tormented her!" Ravina snapped.

"And talented?"

"Her singing in the Chums Corner Community Theatre production of *Madame Butterfly* put Maria Callas to shame."

"Were you present when your tormented, talented mother brutally stabbed your unsuspecting father to his grisly death?" Bugg inquired.

"I was," Ravina stated.

"Would you tell the court everything you can recall about the incident, Miss Varnish?"

"If you want, sure," she said, trying in vain to adjust her body to the brutally uncomfortable chair. "We were all lounging in the living room, watching *Tic Tac Dough*. My father told my mother that he had a tough day at work, a nagging headache, and four other wives. Then she asked him if he wanted a juicy slice of watermelon and he said yes. I said yes, too, even though she hadn't asked me, but I was an enthusiastic little tyke, and a piece of watermelon sounded perfect after a Salisbury steak frozen dinner. So, the three of us marched into the kitchen, and on the Formica table was a long, sharp butcher knife."

Ravina took a moment to collect herself.

"Please proceed," Bugg said.

"Mommy picked up the knife and plunged it into Daddy's chest. Before pulling it out, she rotated it clockwise till it made a full circle. Then she pulled it out and did it again, this time in a different part of the chest. She said she was trying to locate his heart. Five stabs later, she said, 'I forgot. The bastard doesn't *have* one.'"

The jury was listening with bated breath.

"Because of this unconventional incident," Bugg stated, "you grew up thinking murder was an acceptable act, didn't you? Would you consider yourself an upstanding citizen? Are you someone who respects the law, or do you take it into your own hands? Tell me, Miss Varnish, do you know right from wrong?"

"No, yes, yes, no, and yes," Ravina said.

"You grew tired of Moose McGill, didn't you! But he didn't let you move on to the *next* bad boy! So you decided to slaughter the man who stood in your way, the powerful, omnipresent pissant who prevented you from pursuing other punks."

"No!" Ravina shouted.

"Yes!" Bugg bellowed. "Yes! A thousand times yes! No further questions at this time."

The general consensus was that Ravina would be found guilty of murder in the first degree and sentenced to a long, tedious, interminable life behind bars with food from hell, even on Thanksgiving.

But at the final hour, Dolores McGill Miranda took center stage and delivered an emotional, overwhelming closing statement that mesmerized all who were present.

"If the defendant was represented by another attorney, that attorney would now call upon yours truly to take the stand," Dolores explained. "But since I cannot cross-examine myself, I will speak to the members of the jury directly."

She turned and faced the five men and seven women chosen to decide the fate of Ravina Varnish. "I am the sister of Moose McGill. It startles me, it actually makes me shudder, literally, to think that I'm his blood relative. If I didn't know our parents, I would've guessed that Moose had been born of a human and a jackal. But I *did* know our mother and father, and it's necessary for *you*, my fellow citizens, to know them too, in order to understand what made Moose McGill the monster he was."

Dolores took a gigantic breath. "Norman and Marionette were their names. It was obvious that they didn't want offspring, but a sweet baby girl came along, *me,* and then a demon baby boy, *Moose.* Did they change their lifestyle to suit these tots? Unfortunately not. When Moose was an infant, I remember my father cramming him into the freezer to cool his temperature."

A member of the jury gasped.

"I became accustomed to seeing a glass in my mother's hand from early morning until late at night, always wondering why she was so thirsty. When I was around five, I recall her telling me that red wine was a fruit drink. My father guzzled straight from the bottle. They shirked their parental responsibilities to such a degree that food was often sacrificed for booze and drugs.

I'm proud to say that my goal was to escape my horrific home environment and *make* something of myself. Moose's goal was to escape his horrific home environment and seek revenge on the world. *That* he did. My brother became a career criminal, holding up convenience stores, burglarizing nursing homes, and beating up transvestites to steal the cash from their designer bags.

He had absolutely no regard for life, human or otherwise."

Dolores took a moment to gaze at Ravina with a tender smile. "Ravina Varnish *saw* something in him, I don't know what it was—maybe the buried innocence of that young boy. I warned her, but it's as difficult to douse the flames of passion as it is to reroute drug traffic through a police precinct. In his own demented way, Moose thought he was doing something *noble* when he strangled Babs DuBarry, chopped her into wee little pieces, and stuffed her into one of Ravina's sparkling washing machines. He thought he was punishing her for her part in the destruction of my greenhouse. It doesn't take a psychologist to see that he was punishing our parents, Norman and Marionette, for the childhood they inflicted upon him. But my demon brother would've continued killing because he was the fifth horseman of the apocalypse following Pestilence, Famine, Death, and Celibacy. Ravina Varnish shot my bad-seed sibling in self-defense, and she deserves nothing more than a verdict of not guilty so that she can return to Ravina's Rinse Cycle and lead a rewarding life of service to her fellow man and woman who, week after week, are inundated with loads of filthy laundry. Ladies and gentlemen of the jury, I thank you."

Waiting for the verdict was an agonizing experience. Minutes turned into hours, hours into days. Luckily, Ravina had support from her new gal pal in the slammer, Paprika Link. Like Ravina, Paprika was the victim of some exceedingly bad luck. Her husband, Silas, had been a professional semen salesman, though Paprika suspected the business was merely a front for fishier activities. After Silas died peacefully in his sleep from a stab wound in the stomach, Paprika took control of the company, and that's when her troubles began. A tall, black fashion model requested the sperm of a tall, black pro athlete. Just for fun—because that's the kind of gal Paprika is—she supplied the statuesque beauty with the semen of a short, chubby, Southern, white Baptist. Well, the model wasn't laughing. Neither was the jury. Paprika was serving a four-year sentence for fraud. The only silver lining was that she would probably get out early for good behavior. And she might be able to adopt that chubby, mixed-race, Baptist kid.

"Don't fret, Ravina," she said. "You're gonna be found not guilty. I feel it in my bones."

Luckily, Ravina had more luck with Paprika's bones than the bones of Babs DuBarry and Montserrat Crescendo. After seven days of deliberating, after an entire week of sheer, nerve-racking suspense, Ravina Varnish was found *not guilty* of murder in the first degree.

Cheers reverberated through the city. Ravina's friends rejoiced. All arrests—petty and substantial—were put on hold for the entire day.

Back at the precinct, Calvin and Ravina celebrated with a flute of the finest French champagne.

"Sometimes our justice system works like a charm," Calvin proudly said.

"Sometimes it does. Sometimes those righteous, upstanding members of the jury fight for the innocence of a human being they don't even know and never slept with. Mankind is wonderful!" Ravina exclaimed. "You know what I'd like to do? I'd like to give each juror a little gift: a Shiseido eyelash curler for the gals and a Make-Your-Own-Hot-Sauce-Kit for the guys."

"That's awfully nice but unnecessary," he said. "It's the *thought* that counts."

"Well, I'm sure *thinking* it," Ravina said. "Oh Calvin, I fought for my life and got it back. Better than ever!"

"Now that you've avoided decades of steel bars, stale bread, and tough-talking broads, what are your plans? Will you return to the Laundromat?"

"Of course," she responded. "It's my home. My customers count on me for the brightest whites and cleanest colors. And I count on their quarters. As soon as I scrub the blood out of the washing machines, I'll re-open for business."

"I hope I'll be part of your new life."

"Listen, I'm a strong, successful woman who doesn't need a man to wine me, define me, or concubine me. But truth be told—I wouldn't mind a little wining from you, Officer Clout."

"Then that's what you'll get," he said with sincerity. "You've taken over my world in an irrational, unprofessional way. Abnormal, unseemly, unreasonable, inconceivable. Totally unexpected and illogical. Nutsy, crazy–"

"I get the idea," she interrupted. "I can't even imagine

such happiness, waking up with a man who isn't wanted in at least one state. But I have a few questions for you."

"Shoot," he said.

"OK. On an average day, what do you do in your spare time?"

"I study the Law Enforcement Manual, organize my closet, boil egg whites, and watch the Weather Channel."

"Holy crap," Ravina mumbled. "Next question: Will you, an esteemed officer of the law, be embarrassed to be seen with me in public?"

"On the contrary," Clout said. "I'll be proud."

"Good." She breathed a sigh of relief. "Will you be ashamed to take me to Christmas dinner with the folks?"

"I can hardly wait for you to meet them."

"One final question. Can you guess what I'm in the mood for right now?"

"I have a general idea," Calvin said, heart racing. He knew what *he* was in the mood for. "But I'd like you to tell me. I want you to say it out loud."

"Exactly *how* loud?" Ravina seductively asked.

"As loud as your lungs will allow," Calvin said, sweating buckets through his white oxford shirt. "Tell me what you're in the mood for. Say it. Now."

"You're about to erupt like Mount Vesuvius, aren't you," she commented.

"Maybe," he replied.

"All right, control yourself," she began, looking him directly in his blue-saucer eyes. "I'd love a big, thick egg-salad sandwich on sourdough toast with sprouts, Gouda cheese, and gobs of mayo. Plus a piping-hot potato knish. And for dessert, a chocolate swirl cheesecake. Not a slice. A *cake*. All I had today was an anxiety salad with a side of fear. Could you go for something?"

"Sure," Clout said, realizing his carnal passion would have to be put on hold. "A bowl of chicken broth and a bowl of lobster bisque."

"Two soups?" she asked.

"When you *like* something, why not drown in it?" he asked.

"I like that attitude," Ravina told him, genuinely surprised by his response. "There may be hope for you yet, Officer Calvin Clout."

"Thanks," he replied with pride. "And hope for *us*."

Winter Blast

Every November, when the first blast of winter strikes New England, Brianna Hewitt suffers a paralyzing panic attack. Gripped by agonizing fear, her breathing becomes heavy, her hands tremble, and her body temperature seems to drop ten full degrees until her teeth rattle.

Seventeen-year-old Skylar Hewitt was everything her younger sister Brianna wanted to be: stylish, smart, outgoing, popular. Plus she had the most hypnotic blue eyes of anyone in the zip code. Basically, she was a goddess. The four-year age difference between the sisters might as well have been four *days* because the older sibling treated the younger one like a best friend.

Despite their closeness, something unspoken hovered between the girls. Every few weeks, Skylar locked herself in her second-story bedroom for hours at a time. When she finally emerged with eyes red and hair mussed, Brianna would ask what was wrong and Skylar would shrug and say, "Nothing. I'm fine." But it was obvious she was far from fine, as far from fine as one could be. The concerned Brianna had no idea where this mysterious dramatic slide was leading.

With that first chill of the season, Brianna is instantly thirteen again, in the bulky winter coat, wool mittens, and cashmere scarf her mother insisted she wear three years earlier on that bitter cold, dreadful day. The sun, shining brightly in the cloudless sky, had lost its power to warm the planet.

On that somber morning, Thomas Hewitt carefully navigated the treacherous New Bedford roads as a moderate snow came down. He was the stalwart head of the family, the strong, responsible one who rarely showed emotion. It was even difficult to get him to laugh. The defroster of the Infiniti was turned on as was the heat, but the radio, always an active participant in a family drive, was off, and nobody said a word. The silence was eerie, unnerving. Worst of all, Brianna wasn't accustomed to being in the back seat of the family car without her sister; she felt like she was missing a limb.

In a black, designer dress and wide-brim hat with a veil the size of a third-world country, Emmaline Hewitt was perched in the passenger seat in what seemed like a stupor of grief, a human mannequin staring sullenly ahead with blank, unblinking eyes. Emmaline Hewitt was all about appearances. Besides the physical (perfect hair and makeup, stylish clothing), her impressive, immaculate house was her identity, her soul, her raison d'être. She delighted in having friends over to gush about a redecorated den or rave about a new piece of art. Ironically, she considered herself the ideal wife and mother when she was actually the supercilious Hewitt ice queen attached to the spotless Hewitt ice palace. As long as the carpets were cleaned, the furniture dusted, and the chandeliers gleaming, all was right with the world.

But now, now, now. Right now, tomorrow, the day after that, and the day after that, and the weeks and months and years to follow. Right now and *forever*, everything had changed. Now that her eldest daughter committed suicide, there was a stain on the glittering palace—a nasty, permanent one—and no amount of dusting or vacuuming or polishing could remove it. Emmaline knew that it was way too soon to discuss selling the house and moving to another town where nobody knew the Hewitt family history, but the thought *had* crossed her mind. Many times.

Brianna didn't understand why her sister had been so troubled. Her grades were outstanding, she had more friends than just about anyone her age, and the cute boys texted her all the time for dates. *What else could she have wanted?* Brianna wondered. To lead such a charmed life in such an upscale neighborhood was the dream of most teenage girls. The sisters accepted the fact that their mother wasn't particularly warm or maternal (and was habitually overbearing), but at least they were able to make fun of her behind her back. The girls had each other, and that was, by far, the best part of being in the Hewitt family. It would always remain a mystery why Skylar couldn't confide in her devoted sibling, just couldn't bring herself to discuss the thing that plagued her most.

The entire town seemed deserted on that traumatic morning, its streets devoid of people except devoted dog parents bundled up in down coats, scarves, and gloves, walking their animals (most wearing colorful canine sweaters), some shivering from the cold. A few agitated homeowners were shoveling strenuously from their snow-enshrouded driveways. The roads were empty except for an occasional snow plow clearing a much-needed path. Slabs of ice were piled upon slabs of snow. With icicles dangling from windows and rooftops like fangs, some of the houses in this affluent community looked more like colossal igloos than Dutch colonials.

At the corner of Quincy and Polk with not a vehicle or pedestrian in sight, the car came to an abrupt halt. Mr. Hewitt shut his eyes and pressed his palms heavily on the horn as if he'd seen a child run into the road. The booming roar bombarded the neighborhood like an air raid siren. Brianna felt *invaded*, and her heart, thumping furiously, felt like it would burst from her chest.

When she opened the car door, she was hit with a blast of frost that stung her face like a barrage of needles. But that didn't stop her from running away from the hideous noise into the snow-blanketed street. All Brianna wanted to do was escape the vehicle of grief, the four-door cage, the claustrophobic tomb that entrapped her. She wanted to forget the grim reality that it wasn't just her sister who died; it was her entire family.

When she dramatically slipped on a patch of ice, her body fell sideways into a three-foot high block of snow as if into a comforting cloud. Remaining there like dead weight was a tempting contemplation. Blissfully absorbing the silence and savoring the solitude, Brianna felt at peace for the first time in days. She wondered how long it would take for hypothermia to set in, and then death. Interrupting these pleasurable thoughts, her father's hands grabbed hold of her shoulders and lifted her with herculean strength. "Come on, honey," he said with as much comfort as he could muster. "Let's go."

Shivering from the cold, Brianna trudged back to the car with her father's strong arm firmly around her. She couldn't feel her feet, frozen like blocks of refrigerated flesh and bone, but she managed to climb into the vehicle and sit, her back slumped in sorrow. The snow was falling heavily now, the flakes as big as flecks of ash from a forest fire. On the blackest day of Brianna's young life, she found herself in the whitest setting imaginable, a whopping winter wonderland without the wonder.

Brianna outgrew the bulky wool coat she wore on that merciless November morning, but the scarf and mittens remain in the bottom drawer of her dresser. She painstakingly avoids the closet; that's where she found her sister. That's where Skylar's life ended, and all the tumult began. The doorbell never seemed to stop ringing. Police officers, one after another, examined the house and asked barrages of questions. Psychiatrists asked different questions. Aunts, uncles, grandparents, and friends stopped by with large platters of food, just what the family needed: meatloaf, macaroni and cheese, deviled eggs, and green bean casseroles.

Sometimes, early in the morning, Brianna is struck with the sensation that Skylar is on her way home and will materialize any moment. She cherishes those few seconds of altered reality, but the truth reveals itself all too quickly.

When a panic attack occurs, Brianna crouches on her bed in her darkened room, her chin on her knees, one quivering hand clasping the other. Sometimes she stays that way for ten minutes, sometimes two hours.

The *now-only-child* struggles through this tormenting ritual just as she struggles every time she sees a pair of sisters strolling down the street, laughing, chatting or simply holding hands. She always recognizes the smile on the younger one's face, the expression of pure contentment. Joy taken for granted.

And then it happened.

Her fifteenth birthday was just around the corner. The morning before the big day, Brianna stepped into the bathroom and turned on the faucet, just like she did every morning. Then she caught a glimpse of herself in the mirror, and she stopped. Stopped moving. Stopped breathing. The earth stopping revolving. The only sound in the room was that of the cold water gently cascading into the sink.

Gazing at her image as if seeing it for the first time, she registered shock and delight. Astonishment and disbelief. Pure wonder. Without taking her eyes away from the mirror, she gently touched her face. "I look just like you, Skylar," she whispered. "I never realized it, but I look just like you." Overwhelmed by the resemblance, she felt a sweeping sense of joy. From this moment forward, Skylar would only be a glance away.

Brianna resisted the impulse to run to her parents and tell them about her magnificent discovery. She resisted the impulse to run into the street and shout it to the immediate world.

Better Looking From Behind

Whenever Henry Gutteridge walked down the street, the women behind him were transfixed. His full head of wavy brown hair looked like it belonged to a twenty-year-old, the broad shoulders on his six-foot frame suggested a body that was lean and muscular, and the clothing he wore was stylish and expensive. Sometimes these women increased their pace in order to get a peek at Henry from the front, expecting to feast their eyes on the face of a film star and physique of a fitness model. Instead they found someone with the haggard, weathered look of an aging alcoholic.

With skin as pallid as a faded tombstone and circles under his eyes the color of uncooked steak, Henry appeared as if he'd been deprived of sun and sleep for a decade. If they didn't freeze, these females on the street usually pretended they were trying to get a look inside a store window. Occasionally, a shell-shocked woman would just take off, flee from the face she considered too horrible for human eyes. Henry thought this behavior was more than disrespectful; he regarded it as sadistic. Each time it happened, it felt as if his body had been grazed by fire, his skin viciously charred and burned. Henry Gutteridge lived in the scorched body of a survivor.

Henry *was* an alcoholic, a recovering one, sober for nine years and seven months. He was exceedingly proud of this statistic but ashamed that he'd been drinking for more than half his life. Every morning had begun with a slice of melon, a martini, and a smoke. With a respectable job in banking, a decent place to live, and a devoted German shepherd named Valmont, he was a *functioning* alcoholic. The truth was that his loneliness was borderline unbearable. The phone never rang, neighbors never knocked on his door, and his only living relative, a younger sister, had become estranged because of his drinking. Sometimes Henry screamed (with every ounce of energy in his body) into a pillow just to enjoy the sensation of a nearby sound.

After the age of thirty-five belted Henry in the face, his boozing became so bad that he began blacking out at the bank. The second time it happened, he was fired. Hitting rock bottom made him face the stark, unfortunate fact that his life would not improve unless he stopped drinking altogether.

He devoted every waking moment to his recovery—attending twelve-step meetings daily, working with a sponsor, reading books about the disease of alcoholism. Within eight months Henry was sober. Every night, after making it through an entire day without a sip, Henry felt a genuine sense of pride. He even reached out to others to help them with their struggle. But he was still agonizingly alone, experiencing life from the rafters when the stage was miles away, convinced that someone else was living the life he was *supposed* to live, someone wealthy and good looking, respected and popular.

When he first saw the goddess on a crisp, radiant day in September, he froze in his tracks. He couldn't believe how breathtakingly exquisite this woman was. That was the first shock. The second was that she didn't wander away when she saw him staring at her. Her feet remained planted on the sidewalk in front of a popular patisserie as pedestrians strolled by in the wind. Draped in a gray cashmere coat with a diaphanous Hermes scarf wrapped around her neck, this magnificent beauty looked like she stepped out of a more elegant, glamorous era. Henry was ecstatic that she was allowing his gaze to sink into her flawless skin.

She was the first to speak. "Hello," she said in a warm, welcoming voice.

Henry returned the greeting and proceeded with polite conversation. Five minutes into the chat, a strong breeze caused the silk scarf to fly off the woman's neck. Henry bolted down the block in hot pursuit, finally managing to grab the colorful accessory when it became trapped in a metal gate in front of a vintage-record store that had gone out of business. "Thank you so much," she said when he handed it back to her. "It's getting rather chilly, don't you think?" Henry took this as an obvious goodbye, but to his great surprise, the enchantress suggested they continue their conversation at a small bistro a half block down the street.

She spoke with gentle elegance. She walked with charm school poise. Her name was Angelique Ruby. As they sipped hot tea, they discovered their mutual love of canines, the countryside, and art deco. Henry was more than a little surprised to learn that Angelique hailed from Polk City, Iowa, population 4,000. She seemed as Midwestern as Montparnasse. Her exotic name, haunting face, even her elegant, vowel-rich voice suggested she was from some sophisticated European city.

"My father was a real estate mogul," she said. "After he passed away, I sold most of his property, but I held onto a concrete slab of a building in downtown Chicago."

"I hate those ugly concrete slabs," Henry said.

"I don't think *anything* in the world is ugly," Angelique told him. "I believe there's a bit of beauty in just about everything."

"Wow," Henry said. "That's a really nice way to look at things."

When they finished their tea, Angelique suggested they have dinner the following night. After exchanging information via their mobile devices, they shook hands cordially and went on their way.

Overwhelmed with excitement, Henry wondered if too much happiness might be dangerous to his health, too severe a jolt to the system. Then he reminded himself there was no chance of a second or third date with this modern-day Aphrodite. This made him feel infinitely more relaxed.

The next evening, when Angelique opened the oak door of her sprawling colonial home, Henry gasped. Though she was dressed simply in black with a strand of pearls around her neck, she seemed like royalty. She guided him on a tour of the house as her three tiny Yorkshire terriers tagged along on the white carpet. Paintings of all sizes dotted the walls. The master bathroom was larger than Henry's entire one bedroom bungalow. Everything was arranged as meticulously and exquisitely as a window at Barney's. Henry couldn't recall ever seeing a more opulent residence.

After Angelique slipped into a resplendent crimson coat that flowed to her ankles, the couple was off to dinner. She didn't seem to mind climbing into Henry's ten-year-old Toyota with its dented fender and inoperative taillight, but *he* was more than a little embarrassed by the dilapidated vehicle. Still, he drove past the towering oak trees and stately elms of the neighborhood with a genuine smile on his face, grateful to be in Angelique's company.

Inside the elegant restaurant, smartly dressed patrons were enjoying their food and drink while admiring the modern art on the walls. After Henry and Angelique were seated at a corner booth, a flattop-haired server named Seger appeared before them with menus. Angelique went for the roasted filet mignon, Henry decided on the Dover sole.

"What do you want out of life?" Angelique asked as soon as Seger left the table.

Henry couldn't help laughing. "So much for superficial chitchat," he commented.

"I'm not a big fan of small talk," she explained.

Henry contemplated for a long while before answering the question. "I guess I just want to be accepted," he confessed.

"Being accepted is important. That's a noble thing to want."

Now it was Henry's turn to ask. "What was the worst experience of your life?" he inquired.

Angelique also took her time to respond. "I experienced a devastating tsunami," she said. "That was truly terrifying, but it wasn't the worst experience of my life."

"You don't have to say any more. If something was worse than a tsunami, it must've been deeply traumatic, and we don't know each other well enough yet."

"That's a wise thing to say, Henry Gutteridge."

Seger delivered two steaming plates of food. Henry devoured his dinner with tremendous gusto, as if it was the first really good meal he'd had in weeks. (It was.)

Then came coffee and a shared a piece of strawberry shortcake. And then it was time to leave. Despite her protest, Henry wouldn't allow Angelique to split the bill.

After pulling up to the entrance of Angelique's house, Henry began to fidget; the very last thing he wanted was to make an unwanted move. To alleviate the tension, Angelique leaned over and kissed him on the cheek. "Thank you for a wonderful evening," she said. "Maybe we can do it again."

"I'd love that," Henry told her, certain she was merely being polite and had no intention whatsoever of a second date.

The following afternoon, Henry was just about to light a cigarette when he received a text from Angelique inviting him to a charity event the coming weekend.

The text ended with the question, "Do you have plans for Saturday evening?"

Henry chuckled. He had no plans for *any* evening.

This was the second in a series of dates for the new couple. One night they saw a movie. Another night they went for a drive. A gentle kiss on the cheek ended each evening. Henry didn't just feel alive, he felt like an active participant in the human race.

It was toward the end of the sixth date when the relationship advanced significantly. After a tasty dinner, Angelique invited Henry into her house. He sat down, enjoying the embrace of the luxurious, plush sofa as

Angelique dimmed the lights. Then she sat close to him, causing his body temperature to rise and pulse to race. The desire he felt was obvious; it was all he could do to breathe. "I love the fact that you've been such a gentleman, Henry," Angelique said, "but if you want to kiss me, I would kiss you back."

Even with this enticing invitation, Henry moved tentatively. First, he caressed her cheek. Then he brought his lips to hers and held them a half inch away, expecting her to change her mind. But she didn't. She remained perfectly still, eyes brimming with encouragement. The moment was so powerful that the air seemed to vibrate.

When she kissed him, Henry's pleasure spread from his lips down his body like a fever. Trembling, he moved his mouth down to her perfumed neck. He brought his body as close to Angelique's as he could, pressing against her, literally trying to reach beneath her physical beauty, attempting to leave his imprint. Moments later, she took Henry's quivering hand and led him to the master bedroom. He moved cautiously, afraid he would trip on some priceless antique, a gorilla in a rose garden.

Within moments, they were stretched out on Angelique's luxurious bed, kissing and groping like teenagers exploring sexual territory for the first time. In Henry's eyes, Angelique was so exquisite, so delicate that she seemed breakable. At first, he deliberately tried to contain the passion he felt for fear that he would accidentally scratch her skin or crack a bone. But it only took minutes for his nervousness to melt in the body heat, and he felt confident enough to perform with bravado. And there it was—a few moments of bliss, bestowed to an ordinary man by the goddess he loved. She was a fantasy come to luscious life.

Hours later, Henry gently stroked Angelique's arm as she drifted off to sleep.

He peered around the room—the handmade Italian armchair in white leather, the art deco cabinet with its intricate carvings, the red velvet Louis XVI chaise lounge. Everything was foreign to him, but he knew he'd remember every detail just as he would recall every sensual kiss, every magical caress, every part of Angelique's perfect, voluptuous body.

A similar scenario presented itself the following night. And the night after that.

And the night after that. One early Saturday evening as dusk descended, Henry picked Angelique up for dinner. Her mood was joyless, melancholy. "I need to tell you something," she somberly announced. "You might not want to see me again."

Taken aback, Henry tried to reassure her, saying, "There's nothing you can tell me that would change the way I feel about you."

"You're the sweetest man I've ever met, Henry." She spoke slowly and quietly, choosing her words with great care as Henry continued to drive. "If I showed you a picture of myself at the age of ten or twelve, I guarantee you wouldn't recognize me."

"Why not?" he asked.

"I was homely, gawky, and terrified all the time. My mother used to tell me I xwas the ugliest girl in the world."

"That's an unforgivable thing for a mother to say."

"I spent my childhood trying to be as invisible as possible."

"Most childhoods aren't easy," Henry said.

"If Dad had been around more, things would've been different," she explained. "His work took him from city to city. It was a miracle I survived, Henry. I can't tell you how many times I thought about jumping off the roof of one of his towering buildings." For a few moments, Angelique retreated into a morbid silence. "That's worse than experiencing a tsunami," she finally said.

Henry nodded with sympathy. "It takes some women *years* to grow into their beauty."

"But the truth is I didn't grow into it," she stated matter-of-factly.

"I don't follow."

"The day I turned twenty-one," she said, "I inherited my father's substantial fortune. Would you like to know how I spent it?"

"It makes no difference to me how you spent his money," Henry said, idling at an intersection.

"It might just make a *world* of difference." Her hands began to quiver. "I spent hundreds of thousands of dollars on cosmetic surgeries," she said. "Two dozen procedures, head to toe. Eyes, cheeks, nose, lips, hair, breasts, waist. Every single part of me is fake, Henry. Nothing original is left."

Henry fell silent. There were just too many thoughts to gather.

"I'm a phony," she continued, "a total fraud. My name isn't even Angelique Ruby. I changed that, too. I was born Ada Ripp," she admitted. The car was her own personal confessional.

"I'll tell you what this proves," Henry finally said. "It proves that despite your upbringing, you molded yourself into something magnificent. An insecure girl can overcome a cruel, unloving mother and become a sophisticated, caring human being. This is a lesson for everyone."

"Take some time to think about this, Henry. I have one final surgery, next Friday."

"What more are you doing to yourself?" he asked incredulously. "You're perfect the way you are."

"I'd like to be as attractive as possible for *as long as* possible."

"You'll always be beautiful to me."

"Six days, Henry," she told him, ignoring the compliment. "There's a lot for you to think about."

"Would you let me drive you to the procedure?" he asked.

"That would be nice," she told him as he pulled into the parking lot of a popular French restaurant in the area. At that moment, Angelique understood exactly what Henry was: a distillation of kindness, goodness, and sensitivity bottled in human form.

Henry dreaded Friday the way a small child might dread his first day of school. The previous week he smoked almost continuously, one pack of cigarettes after the next. When Friday morning arrived, a thick blue-gray fog hung in the air, and rain seemed likely. With Angelique in the passenger seat, Henry cautiously navigated the road. A light drizzle gradually turned into a rainstorm, and the car's flimsy windshield wipers, squawking away, could barely keep up. "I took the entire week to think about the situation, Angelique," he said.

"And?" she asked.

"And I don't feel the least bit differently about you."

Touched, Angelique managed a weak smile.

After driving for forty-five tense minutes with the frightening feel of the road rumbling beneath them, Henry pulled into a parking spot near the entrance of the medical facility. The rain had stopped, but ominous gray clouds hovered. Hand in hand, the couple marched purposefully toward the two-story brick building as if defying the darkness above them.

Dr. Avery Stafford and his nurse Nadine greeted Angelique. "Are you ready for us?" the doctor asked.

"Ready as I ever will be," Angelique said.

Henry was told that the surgery and immediate recovery period would take approximately two hours, so Angelique suggested he catch a movie at the cineplex they'd passed on the way to the facility.

"Good idea," Henry said as he embraced her warmly. Then the love of his life cupped his face with her hands and gently kissed his lips.

The movie, a thriller, was less than thrilling. When it ended, Henry raced back to the medical center and took a seat in the waiting room. He attempted to read a magazine, but he couldn't concentrate; the words all blended together. He shifted uncomfortably in his chair. Ten agonizing minutes later, Dr. Stafford entered the room with an unnervingly grim expression. Henry remembers little of what followed.

"What's wrong?" he asked.

"Come with me," the doctor quietly ordered.

Henry followed him to a small, nondescript room a few yards down the hall. "What happened? How is she?" he asked, panicked.

Dr. Stafford peered out the window while taking a

long, deep breath. "Whenever a patient undergoes anesthesia," he explained, "there's a risk."

"A risk," Henry repeated. "What *kind* of risk? What are you telling me?"

"Complications due to anesthesia are extremely rare, but they do happen. We did our best," Dr. Stafford reported, "but unfortunately she didn't wake up."
"What do you mean she didn't wake up? I want to see her." Suddenly he felt so dizzy that he actually thought he might pass out.

"The patient had extremely high blood pressure, were you aware of that?" the doctor asked. Henry didn't respond. "We inserted a breathing tube into her windpipe, but it didn't work quickly enough. It should have worked instantly." The silence in the room was unbearable. "We did everything we could."

"Can I see her please? I want to see Angelique," Henry said, gripping the edge of the desk to avoid losing his balance.

Angelique Ruby, or Ada Ripp as her chart read, had died on the operating table. There was nothing Henry could do to bring her back.

*

The world of Henry Gutteridge collapsed like an inflated balloon punctured by an ice pick. He barely ate, barely slept, rarely stepped outside for a breath of fresh air. His home was a tableau of sloppiness: sink filled with dirty dishes, bed strewn with sheets half-fallen to the floor, chairs overflowing with unwashed laundry. A miasma of sweat and cigarette smoke hung in the air.

Once again, Henry was alone in a cold, dark universe, this time locked inside his grief. When he imagined his future, he saw dismal nights of solitude with nothing to look forward to. Life without Angelique no longer seemed like life. He became lazy. Listless. Indolent.

One gloomy afternoon, Henry ventured outdoors. In his clunky old boots, he ambled through gray sludge that only a day earlier had been pillows of glistening white snow. He made his way past shattered pines, skeletal trees, and a once-popular restaurant that had been condemned by the Board of Health. Then he found himself standing in the liquor section of the supermarket. Henry could feel his heart race; he was immersed in an oasis that could provide him an escape from the daily hell of life without Angelique.

The bottles shimmered brilliantly under the fluorescent light. One in particular, with its ornate silver packaging, seemed as if it had been designed for a king. He picked it up. It promised a satin flow across the palate, and Henry wondered what satin actually tasted like.

With enormous willpower, he placed the bottle back on the shelf and raced away.

Exactly two weeks after her death, Henry received a letter from Angelique's attorney along with a copy of her last will and testament. The letter stated that Angelique had legally changed the document just days before her passing.

Angelique left everything to *Henry*—the palatial home, the bank account, the office building in Chicago, as well as the possessions he hadn't known about—a white Rolls-Royce, a townhome in Telluride, a yacht in Sag Harbor. All of it now belonged to Henry Gutteridge.

The change was baffling, bewildering, and gradual. It took a long while for Henry to accept the fact that Angelique wanted him to enjoy a more comfortable, more upscale lifestyle. When he finally did, he purchased a modest two-story home and Land Rover Discovery Sport big enough to fit Valmont, Angelique's three Yorkshire terriers, and the two additional dogs he rescued from the pound now that he had a huge, rolling backyard.

Then he learned the unfortunate lesson.

A man whose face could frighten a child, a man who would never look as good from the front as he did from the back, suddenly became the most popular man in theneighborhood, an absolute magnet for women. The moment they learned his address or saw the car he drove, they were hooked. It never failed: Whenever Henry ventured out on a Friday or Saturday evening, he found himself surrounded by a sea of attentive females.

Henry decided to spend most of his Friday and Saturday nights at home, playing with his high-spirited family of hounds and cherishing every moment he'd spent with Ada Ripp.

The Strange Events of Senior Year

There was no explaining the gruesome trend that grabbed hold of high school seniors in the small scenic town of Solon Springs, Wisconsin in the middle of an unusually mild winter. One season earlier, national news was made by a rash of sophomore suicides that plagued a prestigious Ivy League university. Baffled parents in Wisconsin now wondered if this had inspired their teenage children to devise their own original take on that morbid series of events.

The victim of the first shocking incident was Sherman Quisenberry, an above-average student who worked part time at the Dairy Queen and sang in the church choir. His body was discovered on a quarter-mile stretch of Highway 53 that narrowed to a single lane going north and a single lane heading south. The Greyhound bus that struck him was travelling twenty miles per hour above the speed limit, but this seemingly significant fact didn't faze the citizens of Solon Springs. It was commonplace for anyone traversing that stretch of lonesome highway to exceed the speed limit.

Still, the tragedy was major news. Despite the fact that traces of marijuana were found in the boy's system, the residents of Solon Springs mourned the loss of Sherman Quisenberry as if he'd been a member of their immediate family.

The next tragic incident occurred precisely ten days after the first. The body of Priscilla Swanson was discovered on the same desolate stretch of highway that claimed Sherman Quisenberry. Soft-spoken and shy, Priscilla loved hot cocoa, Elvis, and cutting herself. She had a habit of puncturing her pale skin, small areas on her arms and legs. She claimed these were accidental wounds, but the wise kids knew better. The Greyhound bus that ran her down had been roaring along the road at fifteen miles per hour above the speed limit.

Both Sherman and Priscilla were kind, quiet, introspective, and didn't draw unnecessary attention to themselves (except when Priscilla displayed a new bandage), so when the body of the third victim, Andrew "Grunt" Galloway, was discovered ten days after Priscilla's, the authorities were confounded. This notorious "bad boy" didn't fit the mold. Cocky and tall, he swaggered down hallways, skipped important tests, and propositioned the pretty girls who occasionally said yes. According to colleagues, Grunt was always a little high, a little stoned, a little confused. The Greyhound bus that hit him had been zooming down Highway 53 at ten miles per hour above the speed limit.

There were only a handful of lampposts dotting that particular stretch of Highway 53, each exploding in a burst of yellow phosphorescence, but the light faded forty feet from its source, so the area was dark. Not that there was anything to see. Nothing grew, nothing thrived, there was no scenery to admire, not a solitary shrub.

But after the third tragic incident, the people of Solon Springs gave the region a major makeover. Now the region resembled a veritable arboretum with roses, tulips, hydrangea, lilies, and orchids lining the highway for what seemed like miles.

The town flew into an absolute frenzy when the body of Evan Smiley was found ten days after Grunt's. Evan was an outstanding student and an affable guy primarily known for his musical ability and garish socks. He taught himself how to play the piano and the guitar, and he was often asked to perform at local functions. The Greyhound bus that hit him had been moving down Highway 53 at five miles per hour above the speed limit. Traces of rum and Coke were found in his system. On the night of his death he'd been wearing a new pair of bright orange socks with small brown alligator figures.

Teachers were instructed to discuss these tragedies in their classrooms. Parents were urged to speak candidly to their teenage children, to remind them that suicide is a permanent solution to a temporary problem. A grief counselor from Madison was hired to appear at the high school every Monday and Friday. Black funeral dresses were in such demand that Ella of Ella's Boutique had run out. It became commonplace for small groups of women to drive to Chippewa Falls, enjoy a tasty lunch at the local French restaurant, then shop for funereal garb at the popular Fashion Bug. These ladies made an afternoon of it.

High school principal Sidney Tomkins called a special assembly, mandatory for all students. Standing on the stage of the auditorium, he read the mission statement of the Solon Springs Area Unified School District: "In partnership with our great community, we are committed to excellence, empowering and challenging all students to learn while preparing them for an ever-changing global society." These words were met with scattered applause, mostly by teachers and cafeteria workers. Tomkins scanned the blank faces of the students. "If any of you is unhappy about something, my door is open. If you don't like the lunches we serve, if you think our fitness equipment should be upgraded, if you're having a problem at home, I'm available day or night."

"Fitness equipment?" Gail Reinjohn whispered to Marshall Calabrese who was sitting next to her in the back of the auditorium.

"Pathetic," Marshall replied. "He doesn't have a clue."

"He probably spanks his kids with a belt."

The principal continued. "You're at an age when you're trying to make sense of the world, and it doesn't make much sense." These words elicited a few tepid laughs. "But death is not an option. Even if your problems seem insurmountable, you have to face them. You can't decide to skip the hard part. The hard part is what develops character."

"What developed *his* character?" Marshall whispered to Gail.

"They forgot to *give* him any," she whispered back.

"In the early 1960s, sacks of undelivered mail were discovered in the home of a Chicago postal worker," the principal continued. "He was just too lazy to deliver it.

Over the years, as you can imagine, the bills and letters and magazines piled up. The man was a failure. But did he kill himself? No. He just ignored his responsibilities. Well, you can ignore them for so long, but eventually they catch up and begin to eat away at you. So, I'll reiterate my invitation. The door to my office is always open. Please talk to me or to Mrs. Muggeridge, our counselor, if you have any kind of problem or issue. And do it *before* the problem starts to eat away at you."

When the assembly ended and the students began to disperse, Gail and Marshall decided to have a quick bite.

"The adults are in such shock," Gail said over a garden salad. "Did your parents talk to you?"

"Nah," he said over a well-done cheeseburger. "They never talk to me unless it's to tell me to stop practicing the trumpet."

"My mother asked me if I knew any of the kids," she said with incredulity. "The seniors at Solon Springs High are killing themselves. I'm a senior at Solon Springs High. Does she think there are two million of us?"

"Did you tell her they were all in McKenna's class?"

"No."

"It's only a matter of time," Marshall said. "You know, that story about the mailman Tomkins told made no sense. If the guy had killed himself, it would've been relevant. But he didn't. So what was the point of the story?"

"I agree!" she exclaimed. "It only made sense to the kids who want to be mailmen. Then Tomkins gave them an excellent suggestion how *not to* do your job."

Marshall laughed and Gail joined in. She found him to be immensely likeable and terribly hot, but she suspected he was gay. He never made a pass at her, didn't like football, and ate low-fat yogurt. In any case, she felt safe and comfortable with him.

Ten days after Evan's body was found, the bodies of Melinda Early and Davis Spainhower were discovered side by side on Highway 53. This double suicide, the first of its kind in Solon Springs, stunned the already unnerved community. The two seniors had been dating for over six months, and the relationship seemed to be getting serious. Rumors that Melinda was pregnant were quickly denied.

"They had their whole lives," Melinda's mother sobbed to a reporter. "I can't understand it."

"This has got to stop!" Elena Kroll declared to the rolling camera of the local news station. "We're losing our children and we don't know why. Someone has to know why. Whoever you are, please talk to us!" Elena's two daughters were only nine and seven, but she wanted this suicidal trend to stop before they entered their teens.

When Gail heard the news, she immediately called Marshall. "What's wrong?" he asked.

"I don't know if I can deal with this anymore," she said in tears.

"Meet me at the benches near the bookstore in ten."

"Fine," she told him. Even though she lived only five or six minutes from the bookstore, Gail grabbed her wool coat and headed out the door. She was restless; she couldn't sit still.

The air was cold. In fact, the temperature was the lowest it had been all winter. She reached for her gloves in the side pockets. The left glove was in the left pocket, but the right pocket was empty. She glanced behind her to see if it had fallen to the ground. She checked all pockets thoroughly. The right glove was gone, and she was going to have to deal with it.

When Gail arrived at the benches, Marshall wasn't there, so she paced. She tried to imagine how her family would react to her own suicide. Her parents would never get over it, Gail thought. They would be utterly destroyed for the rest of their lives. Her little brother wouldn't understand, but when he got older he would be deeply sorry that he no longer had a sister.

Marshall walked quickly toward the pacing girl. "Hey," he said.

"Hey," Gail responded. "She was pregnant, you know."

"I thought they said she wasn't."

"They said she wasn't, but she *was*. Janet Arliss told me. She was Melinda's BFF."

"Shit," Marshall whispered.

"Look, I don't believe a fetus is a baby," Gail stated with conviction. "A fetus is a fetus and a baby is a baby. But still, there was something growing inside her, and it was on its way to becoming a baby. And the notion of killing that along with herself is just overwhelming to me. I can almost understand how she could kill herself, but not the fetus."

"I hear you loud and clear."

"This is insanity because I am so pro-choice. Why am I upset?" she cried.

"You just are. We're all in a little bit of shock and we react in unexpected ways."

"What the hell is going on?"

"I'm not sure. But it's pretty shitty." He took a deep breath, tried to focus. "How about a movie later?"

"I'm so not in the mood."

"That's exactly why we should go."

Light snow flurries began to fall while Marshall and Gail were in line at the local movie theatre.

"Two for the Tarantino film," Marshall said to the alarmingly thin young woman at the ticket booth. She was skinny in the way only a drug addict or a bulimic is skinny. Bordering on skeletal. Gail dug into her bag, but Marshall said, "I got it."

"Thanks," she replied. She honestly hadn't expected him to pay, and this made her wonder if Marshall was straight and this was an actual date.

When they strolled into the theatre, the lights were still on and the screen was blank. "Where do you like to sit?" Gail asked.

"Aisle seat, like on an airplane."

They took two seats in the third-to-last row. "I prefer window," Gail offered.

"You want to move?" he asked with a straight face.

"I think all the window seats are taken."

"We could ask a flight attendant if anyone wants to switch."

"You say everything with such a straight face," Gail remarked. "Do some people think you're being serious?"

"Yeah. I don't hang out with them."

The lights slowly began to dim.

"Who do you miss the most?" Gail asked out of the blue.

The question instantly changed the carefree mood. "Evan. He was a cool guy."

"Oh yeah, you were friends, right?"

"We hung out sometimes."

"He was so great on the guitar."

"And he taught himself. He was a fucking genius." Marshall recalled the first time he heard Evan play. It was in Stuart Le Sage's basement, and the half dozen kids in attendance were truly impressed. "Who do *you* miss?"

Gail took a moment to think. "Priscilla Swanson, I

guess."

"It wasn't true about her being related to the Swanson TV dinner family, right?"

"Right," Gail said. "I have no idea who started that idiotic rumor."

"I think it might've been *me*," Marshall confessed.

Gail chuckled. "Why do I believe that?"

The coming attractions were lame, but the movie was engrossing. Afterward, Gail and Marshall walked slowly in the brisk night air. The snow had stopped falling, and only bits of it were still on the ground, looking as if sections of the town had been salted by the sky. The clouds appeared frosty.

Gail peered into Marshall's eyes. "Can I ask you a personal question?"

"I'm not gay."

A warm grin brightened her face. "Cool," she said.

In the following morning's newspaper, a front-page article stated that the police continued to gather evidence. It was determined that all the victims had been on some kind of antidepressant. There was only one psychiatrist in Solon Springs, but there were seven in Chippewa Falls and dozens in Madison. "Teen suicide is a major problem, not only in our community but in our country," Dr. Laurence Davenport of Chippewa Falls was quoted as saying. "It's a very difficult, turbulent period of life. You must remind your growing children that suicide is not the answer."

Ten days after the double suicide, a group of six sets of distraught parents decided to be proactive. At eight p.m., they drove to the lethal stretch of Highway 53 that narrowed into two lanes and parked their vehicles on the shoulder of the road. With them were lawn chairs, flashlights, paperback books, blankets, radios, bottles of pop, cups of coffee, and tuna sandwiches on wheat bread. On the other side of the guardrail, they spaced themselves out so that most of the quarter mile of road was covered. They ate their sandwiches, read their paperbacks, listened to their radios, gazed into the dark distance, and waited. Just waited. A few minutes after midnight, the Greyhound bus zoomed past them, travelling at the speed limit. Not one student was seen anywhere near this stretch of highway. When the big white bus had passed the last set of parents, all twelve adults burst into wild applause. With pride dripping from their pores, they lifted their arms, danced to the music in their heads, and rejoiced. They were almost certain they had saved the life of a Solon Springs youngster.

But late Sunday morning, a devastating bit of news made its way around the community like a fast-spreading virus. The ruddy-faced David O'Shaughnessy had jumped from the roof of the tallest building in town. Despite having been caught stealing expensive pieces of jewelry from the homes of wealthy neighbors, he was well liked by his classmates.

How David got to the roof of the eight-story office building was a mystery. According to one theory, he hid in a bathroom on Friday night and spent the next day prowling around the floors. Another theory was that the security guard had been drinking on the job and neglected to lock the front door. To the people of Solon Springs, none of this mattered. Another teenager had ended his life.

Without thinking much about it, Gail grabbed a piece

of typing paper and a pen and began writing. "The dead students were all in McKenna's class. You might want to check that out." She didn't sign her name. She folded the sheet of paper and put it in an envelope addressed to the local police station.

It didn't take long for Mr. Theodore McKenna to be called into the station for questioning. McKenna, a graduate of Brown, had been teaching science and psychology for fifteen years. Divorced, he lived alone and was considered a personable, polite member of the community. Standing in front of a classroom, he had a charismatic, big-brother appeal. Some of the female students wanted to sleep with him. Some of the male students wanted to play basketball with him. "I understand you dabble in hypnosis," Officer Herbert said.

"I don't dabble in it," McKenna responded. "I'm a licensed hypnotist and have cured people of smoking, drinking, and other unhealthy vices."

"Do you practice this on a regular basis?"

"Not in the past few years." He insisted that his hypnotherapy was strictly separate from his teaching.

The police found no evidence that linked McKenna with any of the suicides.

Still, every student in every one of McKenna's classes was called in.

"He taught science, mostly," Gail told Officer Herbert. "But he had a way of conveying his beliefs in the facts that he taught."

"I'm not sure what you mean by that," the officer said. "Religious beliefs?"

She hesitated. "No."

"Political beliefs?"

She hesitated. "No. Beliefs about life in general, I guess."

"Don't all teachers do that to some degree?"

"No," Gail stated. "They don't."

"Can you give me an example?"

Gail fidgeted in her chair. "He once told us that wherever we are in our lives right now, that's where we'll be when we're forty, fifty, and sixty, that nothing will drastically change, that we're already the people we'll be. If we're stars on campus, we'll be stars in life. If we're misfits and losers, we'll be misfits and losers in life. I never believe much of what he says, but some of the other kids do. Some of them look up to him like he's some kind of guru."

"Why do you think that?"

"Because they *need* some kind of guru, I guess."

The following morning, the local newspaper reported that Mr. McKenna and every one of his students had been interrogated by the police. A major part of the story was that each student who committed suicide was in this teacher's class. All of a sudden, public opinion took on a ferocious life of its own, and McKenna was guilty before proven innocent. The community needed a scapegoat, and he was their man.

Parents forbade their children to attend McKenna's class. Still, some devoted students showed up and McKenna taught them as if nothing unusual was happening in the outside world. As each day passed, the residents of Solon Springs became more agitated. On the tenth day after the previous suicide, people prayed no one would die.

Parents made sure their children were safely at home.

Some parents stood guard all night. The rapid heartbeat of the town was almost palpable. Everyone waited with bated breath for morning to arrive, dreading any news that might be travelling through the community like a snowball gathering speed as it rolled downhill.

When Gail's received a text at nine the next morning, she rushed to read it. "Thank you for the info," she texted back. Immediately, she called Marshall. "Did you hear?"

"No," he said.

"Another suicide."

"Fuck," he muttered. "Who?"

"You won't believe it," she said.

"Tell me."

"McKenna. He shot himself."

"That son of a bitch."

Expectedly, the news spread like fire on a gasoline leak. The entire town was stunned and buzzing. Parents of deceased children were up in arms, assuming McKenna had been solely responsible for the suicides of their kids. "The guilt must have eaten him alive," one parent was heard saying at a community memorial service.

No one would be the same—not the parents who lost children, not the surviving students, not the colleagues of Theodore McKenna. The black cloud that was devouring Solon Springs, the horror that was stomping on the town's very heart, had moved on.

A Superior Posterior

The lights dimmed.

The audience hushed.

Carnegie Hall was filled to capacity.

The audience for *Behind Every Great Man* didn't know what to expect except for the presence of Cameron Ryan, the most famous male model in the universe, primarily known for one particular body part, a part that was featured in the best-selling poster of all time, a part that was insured by Lloyd's of London for thirty million dollars. But what on earth would Cameron Ryan do in a one-man show at Carnegie Hall?

Out of the darkness came a lone, sky-blue spotlight revealing a human posterior, the most admired, acclaimed posterior of any current living being. The audience burst into rapturous applause. (Several members of the audience instantly stood up.) Almost a full minute later, when silence reigned once again but breathing remained heavy, the symphony orchestra began to play Mozart's lively "Sonata Number 17 in C." And so, *Behind Every Great Man* began with an overwhelming sense of freedom and joy.

Cameron Ryan, all twenty-one years of him, stood on a slowly revolving platform, draped head to toe in eggshell white with the exception of his buttocks, which were on full, fleshy display. In extremely slow motion, the platform rotated clockwise. It took a solid ninety seconds to make one complete revolution as the lighting changed from one shade of blue to another: azure, cerulean, cobalt, cornflower, royal, sapphire, steel, teal. On stage left, a bright, magical morning sun was in the process of rising.

When the platform completed its first full revolution, it began to revolve again, this time in a counterclockwise direction to the brooding, haunting sound of Rachmaninoff's "Piano Concerto No. 2." As the lighting changed from cheerful blues to muted browns and simmering grays, a feeling of decline and doom descended upon the stage. Cameron's behind seemed to age in the changing light; suddenly these were the sunken, bony buttocks of a nonagenarian, a fanny suffering from disc degeneration and movement dysfunction. Pure gluteal atrophy. Pure audience horror. On stage right hung a dismal, barely discernible quarter moon.

Not a second too soon, the platform began to revolve in a clockwise direction once again. The colors this time were various shades of red: crimson, magenta, mystic, rose, ruby, scarlet, violet. A rainbow of passion. Accompanied by Bernard Herrmann's haunting soundtrack to Hitchcock's classic *Vertigo*, the butt of Cameron Ryan was back in its full glory. A sculpture worthy of Rodin. A rear of sheer perfection. *Vertigo* was a romantic tragedy about the impossibility of recreating the object of one's desire. It quickly became clear that the purpose of *Behind Every Great Man* was to explore the quest to get as close to the *actual object* of one's desire as possible. For the audience, that object is right in front of their eyes but frustratingly out of reach. (Security is tight.) This section is by far the evening's most emotional, with its bracing agony of defeat, an agony that knocks you flat as you blink away tears. You can hear the audience's sighs, moans, and breaking hearts.

Other musical selections in the show include Tchaikovsky's "1812 Overture" (complete with live cannons), the 1960's pop hit "Downtown," a romantic rendition of "Body and Soul," the classic "Cheek to Cheek," Van Halen's "Bottoms Up!," and the Bee Gee's classic "How Deep Is Your Love?".

Then comes the rousing, stirring, exhilarating Michael Jackson song "Beat It." This piece revved up the crowd to such a high-pitched fever that several audience members, the true keyster connoisseurs, took to dancing in the aisles.

But that wasn't all Cameron Ryan and his buttocks had to offer. About halfway through the show, the set opens up to reveal a startling, breathtaking tableau. We're suddenly in a barren, endless desert adorned with lasers, flesh, sand, and the occasional cactus. And mirrors. Oh, those gigantic mirrors! To see several dozen images of Cameron's ferociously firm, round rump is certainly an unforgettable sight, no matter what your aesthetic preference. A half dozen other nude bodies writhe and squirm in the searing heat. Suddenly, almost magically, a gathering of lenticular clouds in the shape of a flying saucer appears, gradually moving west. Is it a mirage? Is it actually going to bring rain? The bodies follow the traveling clouds, praying for a downpour.

In the show's final third, Cameron Ryan speaks. With candid, self-deprecating humor, he shares his gradual awakening to the lessons of his unusual life. He tells us he considered calling this performance piece *The Butt of the*

Joke or *My Butt Is the Joke* or even *No Ifs or Ands, One Butt*. But in the end, he decided that the show deserved a more serious title. And just what are the lessons he's learned? What can such a young man possibly learn from being known for the most glorious gluteus maximus of any human being in history? He knows that some people are interested in him for one thing only. Those aren't the people he wants to know. He *has* been manipulated, but now he can recognize the signs.

The esteemed critic Vitaly Kozlov called the show "a great work of art that soars on its natural merits." Critic Danila Andrada described it as nothing more than "an indulgent selfie." Others were divided. Some called the show a "class act" while others referred to it as a "crass act." One renowned critic (who shall remain nameless) wrote, "There's nothing here to warrant a production that charges an actual ticket price of more than ten cents." If it's merely an exercise in "showing off," as this critic also wrote, it's certainly a creatively produced piece of showing off. A very odd story is making the rounds of gossip columnists. According to several reliable sources, a somewhat confused (or perhaps deranged) art dealer made an offer to purchase "the sculpture" for an exorbitant amount of money. He didn't realize that Cameron Ryan accompanied the buttocks wherever Cameron Ryan's buttocks went.

Cameron still has the same group of close friends he had when he was an anonymous high school student in Springfield, Missouri. He still talks to his parents and younger sister every day. He never heard of Robert Mapplethorpe. Didn't know the name Jeff Koons—which might be surprising to some people because, like Koons,

Cameron seems to be holding a mirror up to society to reveal its grotesque nature.

Is that the *real* magic of *Behind Every Great Man?* Wyatt Muldoon, the show's director, believes there are many layers to the production, and its grotesquerie is merely *one* of them. Muldoon considers himself a minimalist, though he uses that talent here to maximum effect. This is only the third show the neophyte has directed. The first was an off-off-Broadway revival of *Death of a Salesman* with no scenery. The second was a wildly experimental version of *Porgy and Bess* set in Nantucket. Both shows garnered scathing reviews, but many critics singled out Muldoon as "a director to keep an eye on."

*

Behind Every Great Man ran for thirty sold-out performances at New York's Carnegie Hall. The streaming service Hulu optioned the show and will televise it sometime next year. In a creative move, *Time* magazine put Cameron Ryan's superior posterior on its front cover *and* back. The debate rages on. Is this the presentation of a serious work of art or something much less respectable? Should Cameron Ryan's rump take its place next to Rodin's *The Thinker?* Michelangelo's *David?* Picasso's *Guitar?* There are those who think it *should.* Then there are those who think it's an insult to Rodin, Michelangelo, and Picasso to even *consider* this scenario.

Are Andy Warhol's iconic *Brillo Boxes* art? Warhol defenders believe they most certainly belong in the pantheon of great art simply because it was Warhol who created them. Skeptics say they are *not* art because they're merely a replica, not an interpretation. James McNeill Whistler would have been a skeptic of the first order. "The imitator is a poor kind of creature," he said. "If the man who paints only the tree, or flower, or other surface he sees before him were an artist, the king of artists would be the photographer."

No matter what you believe, it can't be argued that the appearance of Cameron's buttocks in *Behind Every Great Man* (as well as in posters and on giant billboards for designer underwear) touched a nerve. Nationwide, people continue to debate the merit of the career endeavor as a whole. Ryan's defenders are quick to point out that the body part in question is different from other works of art because it's *alive*, and we should rejoice in that fact. They tell us we should watch it evolve year after year, notice subtle changes in its size and shape, and accept its steady, inevitable decline as it moves southward with age. Detractors say that's precisely why it's *not* true art— because its beauty will diminish with time. It will eventually suffer from saggy-butt syndrome and its flesh will crumple, crinkle, shrivel. That will never happen to Michelangelo's *David*.

"Filling a space in a beautiful way. That's what art means to me," said the great Georgia O'Keeffe. If one goes along with her definition, then Cameron Ryan's behind is indeed a work of art because it certainly fills a space rather cozily. Of course, art is purely subjective, and there are those who'd proclaim that the space Cameron Ryan's butt fills is *not* cozy. To these people, the sight of it is anything *but* art. *If Ryan's derriere deserves a show of its own, why wouldn't Angelina Jolie's lips? Or Chris*

Hemsworth's torso? These are the sarcastic questions of the cynics.

Will Cameron's buttocks become a victim of the mass marketing of art, just like so many other products in our capitalistic society? Will the next set of perfect buttocks (there will undoubtedly be copycats) be a product of standard assembly line thinking? Or is Cameron one of a kind? Only time, and the fickleness of the youthful consumer, will tell.

After *Behind Every Great Man* completed its record-breaking run at Carnegie Hall, producers offered Cameron a major international tour that included London, Dublin, Hoboken, Bangkok, Salt Lake City, Paraguay, Boise, and the People's Republic of Bangladesh. His chiseled trunk would become a worldwide commodity and a money-making monster.

Cameron is still mulling the offer. He isn't sure he wants the attention, and that's just *one* of the drawbacks of performing the show. Standing on a stage for almost two hours each night can be incredibly grueling. If he happens to get sick, the scheduled show is canceled. Can you imagine the horror and disappointment of the audience if an understudy took his place for one performance?

Cameron confessed that he occasionally wonders whether he's compromising his integrity. His rear is a bona fide cash cow; he recently purchased a 6,500-square-foot summer home for his parents in Bridgehampton. And he gifted each of his three closest friends from home with a sleek new Ferrari 812 that can go from zero to 60 in 2.8 seconds. Recently, one of them, ironically named Wade Speedman, was driving 64 mph in a 30-mph zone when he slammed into a taco truck, splattering the street with ground beef, shredded cheese, and buckets of sour cream. The sour cream caused a young bicyclist to skid sideways and plow into a pair of nuns strolling north from South Creek Church. Speedman suffered whiplash, the bicyclist sustained two sprained toes, Sister Placid's arm broke in three places, and Sister Restituta hobbled away with a collateral ligament injury. Both sisters offered their forgiveness to the speeding Speedman.

Cameron Ryan is certain he doesn't want to spend the rest of his life as the guy with the world's most famous derriere. The first time he saw his behind on a humongous Times Square billboard, he was mortified. "I wanted to run and hide," he confessed.

Cameron's image no longer makes him want to hide, but he does have other goals and interests. "I've always excelled at mathematics," he states with pride. "Even as a kid in third grade, I was the first in class to master my multiplication tables. I always believed that learning how to divide is learning how to conquer."

His attempt at humor might be tepid, but his passion for math is sincere. He dreams of going back to school and getting a degree.

"Who needs a degree when you're blessed with a butt like that?" asks his agent and manager Benny Liddle, the man responsible for the career of Cameron's rear. (They met when Liddle approached Cameron and his family while they were in line for a ride at Disneyland.) "What makes one behind just a thick, fleshy mass and another a work of art? It's the difference between a filthy little puddle and the magnificent blue Danube, between a paltry ant hill and Mount Rainier," Liddle explains.

"That is such crap," Cameron brusquely barks. "I happen to be blessed with a big round ass. End of story."

The relationship between Cameron and his agent seems to resemble that of father and son. And like all fathers and sons, they don't always see eye to eye.

"You should see some of the fan mail he gets," Liddle boasts. "Let me read one." Liddle reaches for a random letter from a shoebox filled with hundreds of them. He glances at the sender's name. "This is from a girl named Poppy Sue Rucker. She writes:

Dear Cameron, I've never seen anything in the world as exquisite as your behind, and last year I graduated from the University of Southern Mississippi with a BA in art. Yes, art! Your gluteus maximus is a sculpture worthy of Donatello. I have twelve of your posters and they cover one entire bedroom wall. I don't think of your butt as a normal part of a normal human body. To me it's a priceless gem, a rare jewel, and I want to polish it like I would a sparkling sapphire. I want to cherish it. Some unforgettable night I'd like to use it as a pillow. And I'd really love to paint it.

"Paint it?" Cameron asks with repugnance. "What color?"

"No color," Liddle says. "She's painter and wants to paint a picture of it. Like an oil portrait."

"No thanks, Peggy Sue," he shoots back.

"*Poppy* Sue," Liddle corrects him.

These days, when Cameron walks down the street, people stare. Some freeze. Others covertly take cell phone pictures. (He recently caused a minor riot at Chicago's O'Hare Airport.) Still others proposition him with huge monetary offers for a peek or a feel or a full hour alone with this particular part of his anatomy. He often feels objectified, and he understands what women have been enduring for decades. "Society made them sex objects," he states. "I don't mind turning the tables for a while, experiencing what beautiful women have experienced. There are lessons to be learned."

"Such as?" Liddle inquires.

"Nobody should ever look at a person as an object and nothing more," he says. "It's degrading. You can *notice* someone's beauty, even be riveted by it, but then you have to realize there's a lot more to that person behind the flesh."

The notoriety of Cameron's butt has certainly affected his personal life. His most recent girlfriend, an art student, refused to touch his derriere for fear that she might blemish or mar it. "It's a Rodin sculpture," she told him. "I would never touch a Rodin sculpture." Cameron admits he practically begged her to caress his buttocks, but she was truly terrified, and they split up. He's certainly open to meeting someone else, someone who knows nothing about the world of art. An anthropology major, perhaps. Or a woman in politics.

Cameron has never done a butt exercise in his life. He wouldn't know a plank leg lift from a donkey kick. "My rear looks the way it does because of good genes."

And he means that literally. His mother is Jean and his father is Gene (short for Eugene). Would his parents reveal their individual derrieres so that the world could see the origins of Cameron's? "I know the answer without even asking them," Cameron says. "No. Will never happen. Next question?"

The next question is whether Cameron will accept that international tour. At the moment, he's leaning toward turning it down. This makes Liddle more than a little bit livid. "You'll make enough money to last your entire life," Liddle exclaims to his iconic client. "Then you can retire and never look back." Still, Cameron's not sure he wants to face tens of thousands of teenage girls screeching their love at the sight of his buttocks.

"You don't have to *face* them," Liddle reminds his client. "You'll never once have to look them directly in the eye."

The Resounding Sound of Sirens

Karyn Crittenden was petrified of sirens. Whenever she heard one in the distance, she froze. Paralysis set in to such an alarming degree that she couldn't even raise her hands to cover her ears. She just closed her eyes and tried to convince herself that the ambulance would veer off in another direction, which it always did—just as her blood pressure shot off the chart. It always took her several stressful minutes to recuperate.

Never had an ambulance actually been called for the shy thirty-year-old neat freak. Karyn approached daily life so carefully that she never tripped over anything, never stepped in anything, and never fell in love with anyone who was off limits until Roy Engles gazed at her with such intensity that she tripped over a footstool, bumped into a bookcase, and stepped into an almost-empty pizza carton.

This incident took place in the small office Karyn shared with her business partner, Ivy Engles. Ivy was in the process of divorcing Roy because she had come to realize that she was seriously lesbian. Falling in love with Florence Madeira was such a startling, unexpected event that Ivy never could have predicted it.

Now Karyn was falling in love with the husband of her business partner, the reliable guy left behind. A sensitive, bearded giant, Roy had a slight crush on Karyn. When he first witnessed her reaction to the sound of an ambulance, he panicked and assumed something was seriously wrong. "Do you need to lie down?" he asked. "Do you want me to call an ambulance?"

"No ambulance," she managed to mumble. As soon as she could speak normally, she attempted to explain her irrational fear of sirens. "It feels like some demonic entity is rushing toward me to snatch me away and lock me in a dungeon. Or take me directly to hell."

"Hell?" Roy asked, stupefied. It was hard for him to comprehend. "It must stem from childhood," he said. "Some loud noise must've terrified you as a little girl."

"I can't remember any," Karyn confessed.

"Well, we're all afraid of something," he shrugged. "But I promise that I won't let anyone take you away."

Karyn nodded appreciatively, knowing that there wasn't much else Roy could say in reaction to her bizarre abnormality. Still, she believed him. She believed that he wouldn't let anyone or anything take her away. He was like a bulldozer, she thought—strong, powerful, in complete control. And Ivy, with her aggressive nature, seemed ill fitted to him. Two powerful, assertive people in a marriage seemed like one too many.

It was almost as if Karyn and Roy were destined to be together. Roy was remodeling the office, so he was physically present all week. He and Karyn had plenty of time to chat, chomp on pepperoni pizza, and discuss Ivy's surprising new life while she was out taking business meetings.

"It shouldn't be shocking these days," Karyn said. "It's just that, well, Ivy's news came out of nowhere. I didn't even realize there was a closet she was in."

"Neither did I," Roy said, shaking his head. His right

hand disappeared into his thick brown hair constantly, scratching his head. Sometimes he put his left hand under his shirt, and to the casual observer it seemed like he was trying to remove his own spleen. Karyn found these eccentricities endearing yet odd for someone with so much confidence and masculinity. (In high school he was a football hero.) She loved him with a fierceness she'd never known, and she admired his dedication to recycling.

Roy fell hard for her, too. He was crazy about her wavy reddish hair and petite little nose. He loved her quizzical expressions. He admired the earth tones she was inclined to wear—browns, oranges, greens. This made her seem like an active, caring participant in the planet.

Before long, there was no doubt that the couple should marry. They had Ivy's absolute lesbian blessing, and Karyn asked her to be her maid of honor. She thrillingly, graciously accepted.

Karyn wasn't the type for a huge, garish affair. She and Roy agreed to be married at a picturesque local church, warm yet understated with stone walls, a vaulted ceiling and stained-glass windows. Sixty friends and relatives (mostly Roy's) were invited. Felicia and Prosper Crittenden, Karyn's parents, couldn't have been happier for their beloved only child.

The wedding proceeded smoothly, beautifully, without a hitch, until the sound of a wailing siren approached, paralyzing the bride. Karyn held her breath as the noise grew louder and louder with each passing second. She locked eyes with her supportive groom as her heart pounded furiously against her chest and beads of sweat formed on her forehead. The ambulance was coming closer and closer and closer still. Unlike previous sirens, this one wasn't veering off in another direction. It seemed as if the ambulance would crash into the west wall of the church in search of its terrified victim.

Karyn's breathing became impossibly heavy, and then, in her elegant, ivory, off-the-shoulder gown and French-lace veil, she collapsed. Several dozen women screamed. A few concerned guests rushed to her rescue.

Luckily, thankfully, serendipitously, the paramedics were on the scene.

The Unexpected Aneurysm
of the Potato Blossom Queen

As Melinda Wild headed south on North Dahlia Drive, she felt a familiar sense of dread. This was the second month in a row she hadn't read the assigned book that she and her five neighbors had promised to read. At least Darla Nutter had an *excuse* when she neglected to pick up the lengthy Pulitzer Prize winner the previous month; her husband had hip replacement surgery and her fifteen-year-old was arrested for drug trafficking. But Melinda had no solid reason for her lack of preparedness. She just couldn't seem to immerse herself in the social, cultural, and religious history of salt. (The assigned reading was *Salt of the Earth: A Well-Seasoned Journey*.)

The sun was beginning to set, casting pink and gold puffs of light into the darkening blue-gray sky. On an ordinary evening, Melinda would have relished such celestial beauty, Monet's *Water Lilies* up above, but her jangled nerves caused her to feel severely off-kilter. For a fleeting moment she considered fabricating a story for her book club colleagues, but she knew her voice would quiver and her face would turn the color of Pepto-Bismol. Melinda realized one other option existed: She could make the announcement that her marriage had disintegrated beyond repair, and the only reading material of interest to her was a paperback called *Diving Into Divorce*.

This plan certainly had its strong points, but one pesky question plagued her: Was it appropriate to broadcast this jarring news to the women of the book club before sharing it with her husband, Clay?

*

When Melinda Wendt arrived in Kettle Falls, Wisconsin, three years earlier, she assumed she would spend the rest of her life in the scenic community with her then-fiancé Clayton Wild. Dazzled by the rhapsodic rolling hills, charmed with the quaint mom-and-pop shops and the quaint moms and pops, Melinda felt blissfully, uncommonly content.

Prior to arriving in Kettle Falls, Melinda worked in the glamorous milieu of New York advertising. She thrived on the pace and pressure, not to mention the phenomenal perks like being flown first class to Fiji and staying at five-star hotels. But after four years, the intoxication of this glittering life began to dissipate. Dinner at New York's finest restaurants became dull and repetitive. (Often, Melinda would've preferred a cheeseburger and fries to duck à l'orange with potato puree and Savoy spinach.) The duplicity of her coworkers became as obvious as their cosmetic enhancements. The atmosphere was truly soul destroying. Almost as if on cue, Clayton Wild breezed into Melinda's life.

A pharmaceutical sales rep, Clay had flown in from Milwaukee to attend his older sister's wedding to an attorney at a top Manhattan law firm. After checking into the posh Gansevoort Hotel in the trendy Meatpacking District, he headed for the bar where Melinda happened to be meeting a client for drinks. The attraction was instant and intense. Clay was the polar opposite of the pompous guys in designer suits who tried to impress her with their penthouses and portfolios. (He didn't have a penthouse and he kept his portfolio private.) The man was refreshingly down-to-earth. As an added bonus, he had the most penetrating emerald-green eyes Melinda had ever seen. His gaze melted her.

They spent every possible moment in each other's arms until it was time for Clay to fly back to the Midwest. After sharing the most romantic breakfast of their lives, Melinda insisted on accompanying Clay to the airport. He held her hand the entire way, easing a bit of the tension, but Melinda still felt as if the taxi were taking her to a stint in San Quentin. The thought of saying goodbye was incomprehensible.

The couple emerged from the cab and found themselves standing next to a long line of travelers waiting for a tour bus to arrive. After knowing Melinda for a total of four days, Clay got down on one knee and proposed. When she ebulliently shouted, "Yes, of course I'll marry you," the people in line erupted into exuberant applause. A pregnant woman burst into tears.

From Melinda's eyes, the notion of marriage to this man was pure nirvana.

There was just one hitch. An only child, Melinda made a vow to hold onto her maiden name if she ever became a wife, but Melinda Wendt Wild sounded like the title of an adult film. In the end, the Wendt went.

Melinda Wild had no qualms about leaving Manhattan, and her first few months in Kettle Falls were idyllic. Her second few were less idyllic. By the third few months, nothing in Melinda's narrow new world could be categorized as anything even close to idyllic. Her duties as Arts & Entertainment Editor of the *Kettle Falls Chronicle* weren't particularly challenging (there was no art and little entertainment within a ninety-mile radius) and the charming mom-and-pop shops were getting on her nerves. (She longed for just one corporate-owned retail outlet with salespeople who didn't know about her father's ulcerative colitis.) Plus, she actually missed the cacophony of street noise caused by cars, buses, trucks, and irate pedestrians shouting profanities.

Melinda's restlessness impacted her marriage in unexpected ways. The couple seemed to argue every other night, and their normally robust sex life had taken such a severe tumble that Melinda accused Clay of having an affair, which he vehemently denied. (She believed him.) It was much too early in the marriage for banal routine, years too soon for strained silence and awkward conversation around the dinner table. They had settled into a state of stifling domestic anomie, and Melinda seriously contemplated a return to her bustling, all-consuming, exhausting former life.

*

Pulling into Fern Blandine's circular driveway, Melinda was almost blinded by six sparkling white hatchbacks. Two belonged to the Blandine family, and the other four to the members of the book club: Darla Nutter, Polly McPhee, Berta Lynn Luft, and Violet Cornish. Dusk was beginning to invade the neighborhood, and Melinda knew that Fern was silently (or perhaps audibly) cursing her for being late.

Melinda opened the car door and struggled to pull herself out of her dusty red convertible into the pleasantly cool December air. She was one of the few residents of Kettle Falls who drove a vehicle that wasn't white. This was the single thing she had in common with her next-door neighbor Sable Tully. A former Miss Potato Blossom Queen, the scarlet-haired stunner was born flirtatious. She loved tooling through town in the vivid red Corvette she bought after her husband Rusty was hit in the head by a boulder on a hiking expedition. Whether maneuvering the sports car through twists and turns or jiggling through the neighborhood in tight satin tops and suede stilettos, Sable always turned heads. Word on the street was that she also turned tricks, but this scurrilous rumor (started by a married carpenter whose crude advances were rejected by Sable shortly after Rusty's fatal encounter with the plunging rock) proved to be completely false.

With the distinct sensation that she was walking a plank, Melinda dragged herself across Fern's immaculate front lawn to Fern's immaculate front door, which always seemed freshly painted. Before she had a chance to knock, the door flung open and Fern appeared, reeking of some floral scent. "You're twelve minutes late," she said with the subtlety of an infomercial.

"Darn it, I was aiming for eleven," Melinda responded. "Did you have to put on the *entire* bottle of perfume?" she inquired as she stepped into the immaculate house. "*Half* would have sufficed, hon."

A platter of buttermilk berry muffins sat untouched on a small buffet table. Next to it was a loaf of sesame banana bread, and next to that was an orange poppy seed pound cake. "Help yourself," Fern told Melinda. "None of this is gluten-free, so if you have celiac disease you're plain out of luck."

Lounging on a leather recliner with her knees against her chest, Polly McPhee looked like a radiant flower about to bloom. She motioned for Melinda to grab the chair beside hers. Smart, savvy, and sarcastic, Polly was Melinda's one and only true friend in Kettle Falls. "You don't look right," she whispered into Melinda's left ear.

"You're right, I'm wrong," she replied as she sank into the chair. "Terribly, terribly wrong."

"Tell me."

"Not here."

"What did you think of the book?" Fern asked, getting the meeting going at full speed. Suddenly an uncomfortable silence hung in the air like meat in a butcher shop. "Did anyone bother to read it?"

"Maybe you could assign more provocative material," Polly politely suggested.

"I thought this would be a welcome change of pace," Fern said. "Informative and useful. Not the typical *boy meets girl, boy loses girl* saga we've all read ten thousand times."

"I couldn't get past the first page," Darla confessed.

"I couldn't get past the first paragraph," Polly mumbled.

"There are so many interesting novels on the *New York Times* bestseller list," Berta Lynn suggested. "Why couldn't you choose one of them?"

"In all sincerity, most of them are trash," Fern shouted with frustration. "Junk, drivel, crap. When was the last time you finished a book at three a.m. and woke your husband to tell him how thrilling it was?"

Nobody had the slightest idea how to respond to this scenario. Finally, Berta Lynn mustered the courage. "Did you actually think *Salt of the Earth* would justify waking Stan up at three a.m.?" she asked.

"Look, *you* can choose the damn book when it's your turn to choose the damn book. This month it was *my* turn, and I wrongly assumed you ladies took your responsibilities seriously," Fern roared. "And since when do you read the *New York Times*, Berta Lynn Luft?"

"When was the last time you had a full-fledged orgasm, Fern Blandine?" Polly shot back. The question elicited guffaws, none of which emerged from Fern.

"I happen to be a pillar of this community," Fern decried.

"You're more like a pillar of *salt*," Polly replied, "like Lot's wife when she looked at Sodom."

"I better get you out of here," Melinda whispered as she gave Polly's hand a quick squeeze. She got up and pulled her friend to the front door, grabbing a slice of banana bread on the way out.

Like a pair of jewel thieves fleeing Van Cleef & Arpels with stolen diamonds, the women bolted from the unblemished Blandine abode. "That woman is to literature what Fruit Loops is to fruit," Polly offered.

They climbed into Polly's white Mitsubishi and zoomed away. "She was more obnoxious than usual, and *usual* is all I can take," Melinda said. "Know what I'm in the mood for? Something fruity, with a little umbrella in it."

"We'll go to CPR," Polly suggested.

Named for the initials of its owner, Candice Paige Rooney, the immensely popular restaurant was occasionally mistaken for a trauma clinic, but those who rushed into CPR seeking emergency treatment were directed to the Muriel Miramontel Memorial Medical Center six blocks north. With its romantic lighting and intoxicating scent of french fries, CPR was the town's premiere destination for wining, dining, proposing marriage, and discussing divorce. Melinda and Polly were promptly seated in a corner booth in the back.

"Lot's wife?" Melinda asked with bemusement.

"She turned into a pillar of salt, remember?"

"Like it was yesterday."

"Tell me what's wrong," the always observant Polly demanded.

Slouching miserably against the leather, Melinda took a long, very deep breath. "Where do I begin?"

"Hey there, I'm Misty," interrupted a googly-eyed teenager in a frilly, slightly silly turquoise outfit with a fire-engine red waist apron. Her long auburn hair was pulled back into a braid. "Welcome to CPR. Can I take your drink orders?"

"Pomegranate martini," Polly said. "Light on the pomegranate."

"Coffee for me," Melinda said, "with a dash of cyanide."

"Uh, we have Sweet'n Low," Misty offered.

"That'll work."

"Super," the bubbly gal declared before darting from the table.

"Is Misty her real name or do you think it's short for something?" Melinda asked.

"Probably short for Mistake," Polly said.

Melinda laughed out loud. Then her mood abruptly shifted back to where it was. "I wanted this to work so badly, remember?" she asked. "I gave it a year. Then another. I don't want to be sitting here five years from now wondering if I should hang in six more months."

"I don't want that for you either."

"It seems all I do is wait. But what exactly am I waiting for? Godot? Did I actually think marriage to my fairytale prince would last for the rest of my entire living, breathing life?"

"Some women do," Polly reminded her. "Before I forget, did you hear the rumor about Natalie Drucker?"

"No," Melinda said, her eyes instantly widening with interest. She didn't know Natalie particularly well, but she was so dazzled by the woman's classic beauty that she wondered if latent lesbian feelings were bubbling beneath the surface.

"Supposedly she goes to Oshkosh once a month, rents a swanky hotel room, and entertains one guy after the next," Polly quietly announced. "Pockets a few thousand a day."

"Natalie Drucker?" Melinda asked with utter disbelief. "The woman volunteers at the Red Cross! I don't know if I buy that one, Polly."

"I'm just the messenger."

"Well, this particular message sounds way off."

The drinks were delivered by Misty. On the spur of this moment of discontent, Melinda decided to order a chef salad.

"Listen," Melinda said, "I have something life changing to tell you."

"I'm all ears," Polly offered.

"Good," Melinda said, "because today I'm predominantly *uterus*."

Utterly stunned, Polly wasn't sure how to react to this headline news. "Congratulations," she managed to say. "Or maybe not. What does Clay think?"

"He doesn't actually know," Melinda confessed, subconsciously fingering her wedding ring. "Nobody knows except you."

"When do you plan to tell him?"

"Sometime in the very foreseeable future. Two, three months?" she suggested. "You *know* what this would mean, don't you? I'd be stuck in Kettle Falls for at least eighteen more years."

"Unless the kid runs away from home at fourteen."

"I *knew* there was a bright side," she said.

"I should be a life coach."

The chef salad was delivered, and the women shared it. "Sometimes I have nothing to say to him," Melinda confessed. "I sit at the dining room table and we're eating a delectable lasagna I prepared from scratch, and I have absolutely nothing to say. This man is my husband, and we have nothing in common."

"That's not true. Your hormones are totally out of whack right now, honey."

"Last night in bed, we were watching some nonsense on cable, and all I could think about was this guy from high school, Jeff Shattuck. He was by far the hottest guy in the city. If I hadn't been so damn shy, something might've developed, but I *was*, and it *didn't*. So, lying in bed next to my sweet, devoted spouse, all I could think about was Jeff making love to me. Even the *teachers* drooled over him. I actually think he was having an affair with one of them."

"Doubtful," Polly insisted.

"You don't understand. You saw Jeff's golden skin and you wanted to touch it. You saw his supple lips and you wanted to kiss them. Whatever body part he revealed, you wanted to take it home and worship it. Polish it."

"You're slightly deranged right now."

"You know what I did first thing this morning?"

"I'm afraid to ask."

"Looked him up on Facebook."

"Oh, God."

"Jeff Shattuck is the only living person in the U.S. of A. who isn't on Facebook. Why isn't he?" Melinda asked with more than a touch of anger. "Tell me the truth: Why would he not be on Facebook?"

"Maybe because he doesn't want high school girls looking him up years later," she suggested.

"That is not the least bit funny."

"Are you finished with this salad?" Polly asked. "We should've ordered the french fries."

"One more bite." Melinda took a heaping forkful of salad with as much ham, turkey, chicken, and cheese as could fit on her fork. "OK, let's get the heck out of here."

After splitting the check and leaving Misty a generous tip, they meandered to Polly's Mitsubishi and climbed in. As they approached the main road, Melissa shouted, "Watch out!" The stoplight had just turned red. Polly slammed on the brake as two pedestrians were crossing Impatiens Boulevard. It wasn't until they were directly in the bright headlights that their faces were revealed. "Wow, look who it is," Polly whispered. "Speak of the devil."

"Gorgeous devil in a gorgeous blue dress," Melinda quipped.

Some of the inescapable power of Natalie Drucker lay in the way she carried herself. Head held high and spine straight as a flagpole, she walked with unqualified confidence, exuding a potent sex appeal. "She's so poised," Melinda said with a touch of awe. "And she's just plain gorgeous. I would change faces with her in a flash."

"Yes, she's pretty, but she won't age well," Polly remarked. "Features are too fragile."

"I'd gladly take them."

The stoplight turned green and Polly proceeded with caution. When she made a left onto Jonquil Lane, Melinda audibly gasped. Flashing red lights illuminated the street, portending serious trouble if not major tragedy. Though they were half a block from the activity, Melinda was certain the police cars were assembled in front of her house. "What on earth is going on?" Polly asked as she swerved into a pebbled parking spot. She turned the engine off as an ambulance sped past, siren wailing.

Up ahead, neighbors were gathered on the sidewalk, spilling into the gutter. Polly grabbed Melinda's hand and they headed toward the commotion with stomach-turning dread. Four police cars were parked in front of Melinda's house and the house of Sable Tully next door. A lanky guy in a rumpled white shirt seemed to be in charge.

"Excuse me," Polly said to him.

"Are you Mrs. Wild?" the guy asked, munching on a muffin.

"No, *I'm* Mrs. Wild," Melinda said. "What happened?"

"There was a robbery," he announced with authority. "The robbery was in progress when your husband accosted the cat burglar with his bare hands, and then gunshots blasted. At least five, maybe six or seven. Maybe even fifteen or twenty or a hundred."

"What the hell are you doing, Woodhatch?" a tall uniformed officer shouted as he rushed up to the lanky guy in the rumpled shirt. Officer Kevin Garza grabbed the guy's arm, causing his muffin to fall to the ground. "Lock this psycho in the car, would you?" he called out to a nearby female officer. "And cuff him."

"You got it, Officer," she replied as she ushered the prankster into the patrol car.

The concerned law enforcer turned to the ladies. "I'm so sorry. He's harmless, just a little off his rocker."

"What he said isn't true?" Melinda asked, confused and dumbfounded.

"I don't know what he told you, but I'm happy to inform you that your husband is alive."

Melinda felt a gigantic surge of joy and relief. "Oh, thank goodness."

"Facts are a little fuzzy, but this is what we know so far. Clayton Wild was having a drink with Sable Tully in her dining room. Sable passed out and fell to the floor. Clayton rushed to the landline in the living room and called an ambulance. As he ran back to Sable, he tripped and hit his head on a stone statue of her that looks like she was in some kind of pageant."

"Potato Blossom Queen," Melinda mumbled.

"Did you know she has a life-size statue of herself?" Garza asked.

Melinda stared at the officer. "I can't say that I did."

"It fell on the floor along with your husband. He either hit his head on the statue itself or the hardwood floor, maybe both. We think the potato might've struck the back of your husband's skull once he was on the ground. He's on his way to the Muriel Miramontel Memorial Medical Center."

As she stood motionless on the grass, operating in a fugue state, countless questions formed in Melinda's mind. "A potato struck my husband's skull?"

"Very possibly, ma'am."

"How do you know they were drinking?" she asked.

Garza hesitated. "There were two glasses of Scotch on the table," he said with a doleful expression, despising this part of his job. "You're welcome to go inside and take a peek. You can also see a pool of your husband's blood, if you like."

"That's very considerate of you, Officer," Polly said before Melinda had a chance to respond, "but we'll pass on that enticing invitation." She grabbed Melinda's hand and hustled her to the car. They raced to the hospital.

Clayton Wild had suffered a blunt impact to the head. Dr. Harvard Nemecek, a Yale-educated neurologist, explained that the patient had lost all motor capability, but with regular physical therapy he would likely walk and talk again. Then he broke the news that Sable Tully had suffered a ruptured cerebral aneurysm, but there was a good chance she'd pull through. "Just in case you wanted to know," he added.

"Thanks," Melinda said. "Is my husband conscious? Can I see him?"

"He's not conscious right now, but of course you can see him," the doctor said.

In what appeared to be an extremely deep sleep, Clay seemed fairly comfortable under a flimsy hospital blanket.

Melinda sunk into a large, cushioned chair next to the bed, wondering why her husband had been boozing in Sable Tully's dining room at dusk. She couldn't help wondering if *she* was partly to blame for him spending time with the former Potato Blossom Queen.

Clay's mother Marge Wild Bore (her second husband Wallace E. Bore died a decade earlier) was a stocky, imposing figure with a sour disposition and the mouth of a Teamster. Because of her helmet of cropped silver hair and her sharp, angular face that had never been introduced to makeup of any kind, she was often mistaken for a lesbian. But this woman loved her men, and she had a colorful collection of them. Of course she loved her son more than anything else, so she drove her dented Dodge Charger from the small town of Pelican, sixty miles south. "I used to be a nurse," she reminded Melinda, "and a damn *good* one. So don't expect me to leave my boy's bedside anytime soon."

Three days later, the very afternoon a fierce blizzard came charging in from the west, Clay was released from the hospital. Winter weather had arrived with a vengeance.

Moving his fingers and toes was the extent of Clay's motor capabilities. Physical therapy would begin shortly. It was determined that a full-time aide was a necessity, and though Marge insisted on moving into the house for the time being, she wasn't against the idea of bringing in another body. "That way I'll be able to attend my Thursday night poker game in Pelican," she explained. Two nurses were hired, one for weekdays, the other for weekends. It was sheer coincidence that they were named April and May.

The home Melinda shared with her husband took on a disturbing new vibe. With the presence of Marge, April, and May, a chilly formality prevailed, and Melinda felt like an uninvited guest. "With the domestic situation being what it is," she explained to Polly, "I can go to New York and clear my head, knowing Clay will be in good hands." Then she modified her statement. "Well, he'll be in *hands*. And I can take care of my little situation before it becomes a *big* one without him ever knowing."

"Is that what you decided to do?" Polly asked with concern.

"Frankly, I'm still on the fence," Melinda said. "But I like having the option."

Upon hearing the news that her daughter-in-law was leaving, Marge seemed much too pleased. "Take all the time you need," she said. "I can handle whatever the hell happens."

Saying goodbye to Clay proved more difficult than expected. Even though his face remained stone still, Melinda wondered if he understood what was going on. With mixed feelings, she kissed him several times and told him she would return soon, though she didn't know if soon meant weeks, months, or ever.

The clouds were thick and churning as Polly drove Melinda to General Mitchell International Airport. "You have to come back, you know," Polly said to her best friend, her eyes beginning to tear.

"Why is that?" Melinda asked.

"Because I need you in my zip code."

Melinda smiled warmly.

Lazy flakes of snow began to fall on the windshield as the dramatic sight of the airport—with its large green signs announcing arrivals, departures, and car rentals—came into view. Heart beating furiously, Melinda kissed Polly on the cheek, grabbed her cherry-red suitcase, and bounded into the terminal.

After making it through security in record time, she meandered from boutique to bookstore to bakery. In the sea of strangers, she zoomed in on a familiar face sipping coffee from a Styrofoam cup. Natalie Drucker, in a creamy-white cashmere sweater and blue silk pants, was leaning against a wall. She seemed to glow like a model or a movie star. When she saw her neighbor approaching, her eyes brightened. "Melinda Wild," she said in her rich, pipe-organ voice. "What a surprise. Where are you heading?"

"New York. You?"

"Oshkosh, but just for a day." Her mass of lustrous mahogany hair cascaded past her shoulders, practically asking to be caressed.

"You're going for one day?" Melinda asked, trying to sound matter-of-fact.

"I visit my brother," Natalie said. "He lives there."

"I see," Melinda responded, not seeing at all.

"He's in a mental health facility," she quietly explained, "and I prefer a forty-minute flight to a six-hour drive."

"Of course," Melinda said, ashamed of herself for thinking what she'd been thinking, annoyed at Polly for even putting the preposterous scenario in her head.

"You have to be there for your family. I don't think anything's more important than that."

"Right," Melinda said with empathy. "I'm so sorry, Natalie. I didn't mean to pry."

"No worries," Natalie assured her. "How is your husband doing?"

"Very well. He'll pull through."

"That's what I heard. I'm so glad."

"Thank you," Melinda said, suddenly lost in Natalie's magnetic allure. She actually began to feel faint. "Do you know how astonishingly beautiful you are?" she asked, astounded by her own assertiveness.

"You're too sweet," the dazzling Drucker replied. "Listen, I'm running late."

"Have a safe flight."

Natalie scurried off, and Melinda wondered if she'd ever be able to face the sultry-eyed stunner again.

When Melinda's plane lifted off the ground, she realized it was taking her farther and farther from Kettle Falls, and her anxiety grew in an unexpected way. She felt as if she'd left something behind, something she wouldn't be able to pick up in a Manhattan convenience store. A major question loomed in her head: Was this trip a temporary respite from her day-to-day drudgery or a permanent one from the life she'd created? With each mile, she felt herself receding into some gigantic void, a vast, empty oblivion with no visible exit. And it terrified her.

She closed her eyes and relived her marriage in her head, watching it unfold like a movie, month after month, year after year. The leading man continued to be the strong, kind person he always was. It was the *leading lady* who changed; she became distant and restless for reasons having nothing to do with her co-star. But he loved her so much that he didn't leave. He had faith in the marriage. He wasn't one to give up. The husband became the hero in this story, and sitting in that tight window seat 30,000 feet off the ground, Melinda rooted for him, realizing she was the only person who could provide him with the denouement he deserved. There was no doubt in her mind that if the situation was reversed and *she'd* been the one whose skull had been bashed by a stone potato, Clay would have remained by her side, catering to her every need. The wise words of Natalie Drucker echoed in Melinda's mind: *You have to be there for your family.*

Somewhere over Indiana, she began to see everything objectively. Allowing Marge to roar into town like a tornado was bad enough. Far worse was Melinda considering an abortion without even discussing the matter with Clay. Plus, she was leaving town when her husband was about to embark on the most challenging journey of his life. This was the man to whom she'd promised to love in sickness and in health.

The flight was relatively short but seemed to take half a day. As the plane began its gradual descent into New York's JFK International Airport, Melinda was engulfed by a powerful, heart-wrenching surge of emotion. She realized, so clearly, that she'd made a terrible, potentially disastrous mistake. The decision to leave her partner in life was the single most shameful, regrettable thing she had ever done.

Still way above the city, the glittering lights below seemed like they belonged to a foreign country, a hostile, adversarial one in which Melinda was not welcome.

Trembling and short of breath, she was the first person to deplane after the first-class passengers, knowing full well that she had more than luggage to claim.

The terminal was packed with people rushing, running, pushing, shouting, cursing, and shoving as if every one of them had taken a few too many amphetamines. Bundled up for a brutal winter, their armor ready to do battle with the elements, these travelers were fierce and frightening as they glided past the banks of monitors and the signs pointing in every direction.

Moving briskly, Melinda made eye contact with no one. She stepped onto the crowded escalator and followed the signs to baggage claim. She stood by the carousel, watching other people's luggage drop like gobs of ice cream from a soft serve machine until her cherry-red suitcase appeared, brightening its surroundings like a fiery sun. She grabbed it with ferocity. Then she jumped on the escalator leading back to the terminal.

Acknowledgements

Special thanks to the following publications for first publishing some of the stories in this collection.

Eclectica Magazine
PANK
East of the Web
The Doctor T. J. Eckleburg Review
London Journal of Fiction
Underground Voices
Nth Position (U.K.)

Very special thanks to Jeff Laufer, Richard Gitterman, and Julie Hansen. From Atmosphere Press, I'm grateful to Kyle McCord for his creativity and especially Nick Courtright for his unwavering support and guidance throughout the entire process. It was a true pleasure.

And for inspiration, my literary heroes:

D.H. Lawrence, Mary Gaitskill, Kazuo Ishiguro, Daphne du Maurier, E.M. Forster, Michael Cunningham, Alice Munro, Elizabeth Wurtzel, Ian McEwan. And Pauline Kael.

About Atmosphere Press

Atmosphere Press is an independent, full-service publisher for books in genres ranging from nonfiction to fiction to poetry, with a special emphasis on being an author-friendly approach to the challenges of getting a book into the world. Learn more about what we do at atmospherepress.com.

We encourage you to check out some of Atmosphere's latest releases, which are available at Amazon.com and via order from your local bookstore:

Interviews from the Last Days, sci-fi poetry by Christina Loraine

Unorthodoxy, a novel by Joshua A.H. Harris

Drop Dead Red, poetry by Elizabeth Carmer

A User Guide to the Unconscious Mind, nonfiction by Tatiana Lukyanova

The Sky Belongs to the Dreamers, a picture book by J.P. Hostetler

I Will Love You Forever and Always, a picture book by Sarah Thomas Mariano

To the Next Step: Your Guide from High School and College to The Real World, nonfiction by Kyle Grappone

The George Stories, a novel by Christopher Gould

No Home Like a Raft, poetry by Martin Jon Porter

Mere Being, poetry by Barry D. Amis

The Traveler, a young adult novel by Jennifer Deaver

Breathing New Life: Finding Happiness after Tragedy, nonfiction by Bunny Leach

Oscar the Loveable Seagull, a picture book by Mark Johnson

Mandated Happiness, a novel by Clayton Tucker

The Third Door, a novel by Jim Williams

The Yoga of Strength, a novel by Andrew Marc Rowe

They are Almost Invisible, poetry by Elizabeth Carmer

Let the Little Birds Sing, a novel by Sandra Fox Murphy

Carpenters and Catapults: A Girls Can Do Anything Book, children's fiction by Carmen Petro

Spots Before Stripes, a novel by Jonathan Kumar

Auroras over Acadia, poetry by Paul Liebow

Channel: How to be a Clear Channel for Inspiration by Listening, Enjoying, and Trusting Your Intuition, nonfiction by Jessica Ang

Gone Fishing: A Girls Can Do Anything Book, children's fiction by Carmen Petro

Owlfred the Owl, a picture book by Caleb Foster

Love Your Vibe: Using the Power of Sound to Take Command of Your Life, nonfiction by Matt Omo

Transcendence, poetry and images by Vincent Bahar Towliat

Leaving the Ladder: An Ex-Corporate Girl's Guide from the Rat Race to Fulfilment, nonfiction by Lynda Bayada

Adrift, poems by Kristy Peloquin

Letting Nicki Go: A Mother's Journey through Her Daughter's Cancer, nonfiction by Bunny Leach

Time Do Not Stop, poems by William Guest

About the Author

Garrett Socol's short stories have been published in several dozen literary journals. His first collection of stories *Gathered Here Together* was published by Ampersand Books. His quirky novel *Tooth Decay* (a story of obsession, attraction and proper flossing in a small-town dental office) was published by Folded Word.

As a playwright, Garrett's work has been produced at the Berkshire Theatre Festival and the Pasadena Playhouse. As a producer for cable television, he created the series *Talk Soup, The Gossip Show, Revealed*, and numerous other series and specials for E! Entertainment Television.